HISTORY

OF THE

WORLD

ACCORDING TO THE

DRUIDS

by

Kim Kacoroski

This book is a work of fiction. Names, characters, places, and incidents are either the product of the author's imagination or are used fictitiously. Any resemblance to actual persons, living or dead, or to actual events or locales is entirely coincidental.

HISTORY OF THE WORLD ACCORDING TO THE DRUIDS

Cover art illustrations by Kim Kacoroski, Phillipe Velasquez, and Masha Tatarintsev

Visit the author website:

http://kimkacoroski.com

ISBN: 978-1-947036-02-4 (Paperback)

Version 2017.25.03

Dedicated to all lights spirits who are still with us

INTRODUCTION

The contemporary tunes in HISTORY OF THE WORLD ACCORDING TO THE DRUIDS accentuate the ability of reader to view history from hindsight, a twenty-twenty advantage denoting perfect vision. Those who don't understand their past cannot move forward, and the same mistakes will often be repeated. Compared to the events which invited the Dark Ages, the songs provide a lighter mood. This matches the dry humor of the characters portrayed, illuminating the dragons with their timely, age-old perspective on the universe.

Chapter One

A WHITE UNICORN galloped across the steppes that stretched into the horizon away from the mountain. The crystal spiral on its forehead captured the rays of the setting sun, scattering the light like raindrops over the terrain. The colors danced in the dry grasses, leaving behind rainbows like little blessings. The unicorn stopped at the edge of a high cliff that offered a view of a sapphire-blue lake. Its rider dismounted and then helped a small boy off the animal. Lastly, he lifted his bride and set her on the ground.

"Your father and I met at Lake Hovsgol," the woman in white told the little boy, who was about three years old.

The boy's father grinned at his son. "We've come a long way."

The bride laughed at his words as she took the boy's small hand in hers and put her arm around the man next to her. Together, they surveyed the expanse of land and water shimmering before them while the white unicorn drank from a puddle of water that had collected in a shallow basin on the rocky ledge. Minutes later, a large golden Sea Dragon and a tiger-like dragon landed on the ledge next to them.

"Oh, what a beautiful wedding!" Elissa, the golden Sea Dragon queen, sobbed, wiping a few tears from her eyes. "You two make a wonderful couple. I don't know why you ever waited so long to get married."

The young boy intently studied the golden Sea Dragon queen who would be his babysitter for the duration of the honeymoon. He quizzically glanced at Ivan, the tiger-like Sea Dragon with the fierce blue eyes. Ivan winked at the young boy as his parents ignored Elissa and became engrossed in each other. Captivated by Ivan's smiling eyes, the young boy left his kissing parents and went to stand beside him.

"Elissa's biological clock has finally started to tick," Ivan confided to the boy. "She wants eggs."

The small boy straightened proudly and smiled with a nod at his companion with the soft, brown fur. In the Dragon flyer tradition a boy was considered a man by age fourteen, and he was three years ahead of his time due to circumstances, talent, and numerous attentive caretakers. Dragon caretakers in particular accelerated a special type of harmonious understanding of the world. Instinctively, Gerwyn understood Ivan's position and felt confident that they both could help Elissa find those eggs in a matter of time. Something about his parent's formalized coupling had brought him into the center again. He examined the golden Sea Dragon queen again, awestruck by her fishlike scales that glistened under the rays of the brilliant setting sun. With the wedding of his parents still fresh in his young mind, he was seeing one of his babysitters in a new light.

"Well, she is very beautiful," he agreed with Ivan.

Joslin, his mother, overheard her son's words and stopped kissing his father, who continued showering his bride with soft kisses.

"Gerwyn, don't go joyriding on Ivan late at night," she advised her young son.

"Oh, don't worry, Mom. Ivan has other plans," Gerwyn assured her. "He wants me to learn how to play the mandolin so that he can sing to Elissa at night."

Joslin shook her head at Ivan. "Don't keep Gerwyn up late."

"Oh, Ivan! That is so sweet," the sappy-eyed Sea Dragon queen said. She had already started to swoon at the thought of a serenade. "Do you know a child's lullaby?"

"Mama, can I play with the baby Dragons when they hatch?" Gerwyn asked clasping his tiny hands to his chest as he imagined the possibilities. "They would be so little and cute," he said dreamily.

Yuri paused in his kissing for a moment and gently nudged his spouse's face back toward him. "Birth control, you're looking at 'em."

"Ahem," Elissa politely coughed as she collected Ivan and the child and motioned them toward a cave below the ledge. Together the trio headed to the caverns beside the honeymoon suite. "Let's leave the lovers alone for an evening."

Gerwyn took Elissa's scaly hand and cast one parting glance at his parents. He caught his father's eye, and Yuri confidently winked at him. Gerwyn laughed silently and reached out for a tuff of fur from Ivan's back. The small boy tossed his head back with a youthful knowingness before carefully walking down the trail between the two dragons.

"Where were we?" Yuri asked, returning his full attention to his bride.

"Something about dragons' eggs," Joslin reminded him as she covered his ear in moist kisses.

"Ohhhh," he sighed.

Chapter Two

It's never too late

For a declaration of

And a commitment to

Love

Tune Reference: *Marry Me*

----Train

THE NEXT MORNING Joslin and Yuri lingered in their straw bed while they listened to the banter between the Sea Dragons and Gerwyn in the adjacent cavern. Having spent a complete evening and morning in uninterrupted silence, they felt blissfully renewed in their devotion to each other.

Joslin rolled over and kissed Yuri softly on the cheek before rising. But instead of heading toward the cavern to check on her son, she wrapped a cloak around her nude body and wandered toward the view at the entrance to their cave. The embers of a fire remained in the pit near the opening. She leaned over and stoked a few coals, savoring the warmth that enveloped her. When she was satisfied with the heat radiating from her body, she turned and stood upright at the cave's entrance. Vegetation concealed the cave's opening from people who might be wandering around. Confident that she could peer outside the cave without being noticed, she indulged in her own thoughts while surveying the terrain.

Joslin took a deep breath. So much had occurred since she first camped at the lake years ago and caught the eye of the man she had admired from their first encounter. Now she could revisit the scene in the arms of that man, and he loved her deeply. Somehow he had gotten through to her and healed her broken heart, which had been damaged by the razing of her parents' civilization. In his heart she had found renewed life and enduring memories of her parents, whose spirits persevered in the life she and Yuri created together.

Joslin folded her arms inside the cloak and paced in front of the cave's opening. So much had changed. Her world was very different from the one that she had experienced with her parents. She gazed down at the loose soil beneath her bare feet. The only similarity was the love they all shared. Glancing back at the bed where her lover remained sleeping, she acknowledged her luck. Luck was something that she had learned from the Green knights who survived in Wales.

Yuri stirred, and Joslin watched him reach for her in his sleep. When he realized that the bed was empty, he blinked and opened his eyes. Joslin smiled at his maneuvers.

"I'm over here watching the sunrise," she told him.

"Without me?" he implored her as he sat up.

Joslin answered his words with a light laugh and toss of her brown hair. She did not want to indulge him anymore. She noticed how childlike he suddenly appeared in her son's absence.

"Come here, my girl." Yuri confidently beckoned to her. He patted the empty space next to him where she had spent the night.

Joslin did a double take. After staring at him for a few moments, she tossed her head again and resumed gazing at the blue lake outside the cave. She snuggled her crossed arms deeper inside her cloak.

Yuri placed his hands over his head and reclined back on the bed.

"Have it your way," he told her. He wasn't going anywhere. Instead he smiled at her, secure in the knowledge that she would return when she was ready. She had left him with that. He laughed in spite of himself.

Joslin overheard his chuckle. She turned around and looked at him again. He never noticed her weighty stare, nor did he glimpse the chagrin on her face. Joslin watched Yuri amuse himself with the ceiling of the cave. Like her son, he seemed so happy with his own thoughts. Leaving the view outside the cave, she slowly took a few steps back toward him. Here, in front of her, was new terrain. Somehow she had become part of his world, his happy state of mind.

She studied him briefly and realized that nothing could change this. Suddenly she felt more secure than when she slept in his arms. Joslin never would have seen this if she had not ventured outside to look at the view from their cave. Sensing her approaching presence, Yuri dropped his gaze from the ceiling and grinned at her as he cocked his head from side to side. Joslin blushed at the sudden attention. He noticed her discomfort and laughed with soft delight. Joslin noted that it wasn't a laugh of triumph, but rather it was one of innocent pleasure, like when her son delightedly embraced a beloved toy that he required for a restful sleep.

Yuri held out his arms wide for her, inviting Joslin closer. She opened her cloak and drew it around them both. Settling into the comfort of his arms, she sighed as he kissed her cheeks and stroked her hair. Joslin realized what she had been missing.

"Stay with me?" he asked her. "Be happy with me."

Joslin looked up and gazed into his eyes. She whispered in a matter-of-fact, calm manner, "I will. You always seem so happy. Stay that way."

Yuri kissed her lips before answering, "I won't change."

"I sensed that about you," Joslin admitted as she returned his kisses. "You passed that on to our son."

"Self-contentment is a happy legacy," he added, nuzzling her ear.

"I know," she replied with a smile. She softened underneath his touch as she rubbed her cheek against his. Then, eyes closed, she commented, "Have you noticed how quiet it is?"

Yuri stopped caressing her neck and stared into her eyes with a delighted smile. "Yes, child and dragons must be doing well entertaining themselves. I think that we taught them a thing or too."

Joslin giggled before she embraced him. "I know. It is one of my greatest achievements."

"Mine too," Yuri whispered, "but we still have a lot of work to do."

Joslin chuckled at his words as Yuri persisted with light kisses. She answered, "I know. It is a tough job trusting oneself and in the goodness in the world again."

"How much time do you think we have before Gerwyn remembers his nursing schedule?" Yuri questioned with a hint of a proposal.

"Oh, probably until mid-afternoon. I noticed the trio hiking around the lake with a huge packed lunch. Gerwyn will do what he can to encourage new eggs."

"If that is the case, then he might even forget his nursing schedule," Yuri observed. "He is a man on a mission."

"He seems to think that he knows what he is doing," Joslin speculated. "Though I doubt he understands where dragon eggs come from. He senses though that he is key to the enterprise."

"He has experience." Yuri, sighed feeling encouraged in his advances.

Joslin relented, "I know. He brought hope."

"We created it," Yuri retorted.

"That we did," Joslin acknowledged, silently wondering how she ever got from point A to point B.

Yuri noticed the perplexed look on her face and sighed softly. He explained with a proud grin, "All it took was a song."

"An amorous song," Joslin replied as she recalled his serenade. "You have talent."

"Thank you," Yuri said.

Moments later, the couple fell asleep in each other's arms.

****

Gerwyn and his dragons continued their hike around the lake. The dragons helped the boy scramble over rocks and logs, occasionally stopping to examine whatever had been unearthed in the process. Sometime during midmorning, they stopped for a snack.

"How do you think our lovers are doing?" Elissa pondered out loud.

"I suspect that they are probably talking too much," Ivan said as he rolled his blue eyes, slightly exasperated.

Gerwyn ignored the dragons' gossip and munched on his wafers. Then a thought crossed his mind, and he pointedly asked the dragons, "When are we going to find those little dragon eggs?"

Elissa blushed. Ivan cleared his throat.

Gerwyn rose as he announced, "You both talk too much. I am going to find them myself."

"Keep looking, son," Ivan encouraged him as he gave Elissa a sideways glance.

"I'll help you, Gerwyn," Elissa offered and rose to her feet.

Ivan sighed, and Elissa nudged him to keep him quiet on the subject. Then she gave him a wink, silently agreeing to a private rendezvous later in the evening. Ivan followed the queen and the boy without another word.

"I was wondering," Gerwyn began in an innocent voice, "which came first, the dragon or the egg?"

Ivan almost fell over, but the agile, tiger-like dragon caught himself. Elissa studied him quizzically. Ivan shot her a terrified look before answering, "The dragons, of course."

Elissa reassured him. "Don't worry, Ivan. Gerwyn isn't asking about the birds and bees. He is asking about the history of the world."

Ivan collected himself and cleared his throat uncomfortably.

"What do the birds and bees have to do with baby dragons?" Gerwyn, asked, fearful that he might be missing out on important information relating to his mission to obtain small dragons as playmates. He stopped and looked perplexedly at the two dragons around him. He was afraid that he would never find his dragon eggs.

"It has to do with the way the birds and bees pollinate the flowers to create new ones," Elissa answered. She glanced at Ivan intently before encouraging Gerwyn to continue hiking.

"Like snapdragons, dragon teeth, dragon mouth, dragon arum, dragon wort, dragon root, and dragon trees?" Gerwyn pondered out loud. Then he resolutely decided, "We must be close to some dragon eggs."

"Right you are, dear," Elissa replied as Ivan seductively rubbed her back while they were out of Gerwyn's view. Sensing the display of affection, Gerwyn ignored them and forged ahead on the trail with a determined stride to discover a nest of dragon eggs.

"Okay. Skip the bird and bees part," he told them. "Just tell me the history of the world."

"Well, it began on a star in the constellation that the ancient Greeks called Draco," Ivan started.

"The Arabs called the constellation Mother of Camels," Elissa interjected.

"That is another story," Ivan remarked.

"Two stories for the same stars?" Gerwyn questioned excitedly. Everyone knew that he loved stories. For Gerwyn, a good story was almost as good as the possibility of finding dragon eggs. He plopped down on the nearest rock and motioned for Ivan to begin the tale.

Chapter Three

The reason why

Love has wings

Tune Reference: *Livin' On A Prayer*

----Bon Jovi

ELISSA RUBBED HER scaled hands together in delight, swooning under Ivan's mystical charisma.

"That is the story," Ivan repeated, slowly closing his tiger-like eyes with a dreamy, philosophical air. "Planet Earth began on Eltanin, which is the brightest star in the asterism."

Elissa began unpacking small cakes from the knapsack that she carried in her pouch. She placed them on a bandanna in front of Gerwyn, still seated on the rock. He grabbed a small cake and eagerly waited for Ivan to continue his story. Elissa tossed some dragon gruel in Ivan's direction, and he started munching on the puffball, which contained a baked mixture of animal parts and plants. She winked at Ivan, encouraging him to continue the story.

"Refugees in the galaxy had finally found a home within this collection of stars," Ivan continued. "They formed two kingdoms. One kingdom consisted of the Purple Forbidden Zone, which became the realm of the celestials. The other kingdom consisted of the Black warriors, also known as the Black tortoises. This kingdom guarded the entrance to the celestial realm.

Occasionally, this kingdom dropped its guard and the warriors would roam unarmed. In other words, when the tortoise moved without its shell, it appeared more snakelike. These warriors practiced a style of warfare that reflected the movements of the Serpentine Federation, which had been destroying the refugees' planets. Some people call this style of fighting aikido."

Elissa handed Ivan a goblet of dragon grog that she had prepared using items in the knapsack. Ivan sipped the grog as Elissa explained to Gerwyn, "My mother served as one of the first winged Serpents for the kingdom of the Black warriors. She was a divine creature from Pegasus. Some creatures from Pegasus served the celestial kingdom and resembled winged horses. When they immigrated to planet Earth, they gave up their wings and evolved into camels."

"My mother was a Pegasus that helped create the protective nebula known as the Cat's Eye," Ivan interjected, languidly closing his eyes. Highly skilled at embracing opposites, the total effect of the dragon's demeanor served to emphasize a point while not disturbing his audience. Gerwyn had continued to munch on his cake while Ivan spoke. Now he turned back toward Elissa and looked admiringly at her, as if seeing her for the first time. Then he looked quizzically at Ivan, whose eyes had opened wide suddenly.

"Who are the celestials?" Gerwyn asked.

"They are the ones who wanted to keep their light," Ivan replied. "The others degenerated and had to live parasitically off the Light Beings, who had to figure out a way to detach from former intimates without collapsing from within. Those who collapsed had to transform their light. Like the red star Eltanin, they became giants compared to others. Eltanin is a red giant star. About the time the idea for a new planet called Earth was conceived or hatched, depending on your perspective, some of the celestials collapsed from the sheer enormity of the project and became Titans. They battled the celestials who had collapsed in a degenerative manner to became gods. Though the gods possessed enough brightness to forfeit their alliance with the Serpentine Federation, they sponsored developing cultures on the new planet called Earth. The celestials who nurtured the spirit of the enterprise called themselves Gaia. They were very happy about it. It wasn't genesis; it was parthenogenesis because everyone was very receptive to the idea. They had nothing to loose."

Gerwyn yawned. Elissa noticed the droop in his eyes and pulled out a blanket from her pouch. She quickly spread it on the ground so that Gerwyn could lie down.

"They stored their knowledge in a sort of library. That way, the Serpentine Federation would not target a single celestial. The knowledge was stored holographically in spheres of golden nebula resembling golden apples on a tree. The trunk and branches of the tree were passageways between the protective gasses surrounding the bodies of knowledge. Some of the gods that had sponsored the civilizations on the new planet stole one of the golden nebulas. The theft changed the operation of the world forever. The gods suddenly had greater access to the refugees on the planet and began to manipulate them. As a result, the Serpentine Federation was able to infiltrate the garden on the new planet. The effect proved disastrous. The human prototypes began to argue, and a new partner had to be created for the male, who decided to stay. The human prototype that left the garden became a spokesperson for the Serpentine Federation. The spokesperson, Lilith, reproduced for the degenerating Light Beings. Chaos resulted."

Ivan watched Gerwyn drift into a light sleep. When he paused for a moment to collect his thoughts, Gerwyn began to stir. Elissa nodded for Ivan to resume the story.

"Meanwhile, the Serpentine Federation infiltrated the ranks of the Titans and began using the spirit of the new planet to destroy the universe. One of the goddesses, Gaia, turned on her son and husband, Uranus, who had chosen to join the celestials. As a result, the energy of the universe was left in shreds. The group of celestial refugees could not create another planet. However, the collective kept Gaia's name, and the original spirit of the planet. So we have two Gaias; one is a fallen goddess, while the other is the enterprising spirit."

After this story, Gerwyn slept deeply for over an hour. Ivan and Elissa used the time off to become better acquainted with each other. After the boy awoke, Ivan answered questions while they continued their journey around the lake.

"What ever happened to the camels?" Gerwyn asked as they walked along the shoreline.

"They were really Pegasuses that adapted to the land on earth. After storing the remaining energy of the new planet as a gas inside the Cat's Eye, the mother camels brought some of the universe's energy to the new planet in a Regulus star sphere. The camels accompanied the earth and water spirits, which were being pursued by aliens associated with Orion and his Dog star, Sirius. Later they helped establish the Anasazi, who were Pleiadians sent to stabilize the planet during changes. Later, they carried earthlings to the planet. Camels transported fleeing Lemurians from Planet Mu to Lemuria, which is now considered the Madagascar region. Planet Mu was located in a neighboring galaxy and Lemuria represented their base station on Earth."

"Where did the baby camel come from?" Gerwyn questioned after he had thought about Ivan's story.

Ivan sighed deeply, and Elissa winked at him. Gerwyn noticed the wink but ignored their exchange. The small boy picked up a few stones and skipped them over the lake. Ivan began, "Everything in the universe begins with a frequency of energy."

"Like the string on Daddy's mandolin?" Gerwyn asked as he watched his stone sink into the lake after several skips.

"Precisely," Ivan answered, puffing out his chest proudly as he recalled his vital role in the event.

Elissa poked Ivan in the ribs before adding, "Your mother's vibration that provided the inspiration. Ahem."

"Oh, I get it," Gerwyn answered. They finished their walk in silence, and Gerwyn saw his parents by mid-afternoon.

"So what are your plans for tomorrow?" Joslin asked her son.

"We are going to look for a baby camel," Gerwyn told her. "I've never seen one."

"Do the dragons know yet?" his father quizzed. Then he glanced at Joslin for her reaction. "You'll have to go to Egypt to find one."

"Only if the dragons agree to go to Rhakotis at the mouth of the Nile River," Joslin insisted. "It is protected by the Cat's Eye energy."

The next day Gerwyn and the dragons used the portal in the adjoining cavern to land at Rhakotis, a small coastal city in Egypt.

"We will emerge through a library that has been hidden in another dimension. During the time of intergalactic wars, several priests cloaked it using the Cat's Eye," Elissa explained. "Alexander, the Persian invader, tried to find it before blocking the opening with his own library. Burning

Alexandria to the ground freed the passageway. His mentors had contributed to the exile of one of ancient Greece's leaders, Pericles. Pericles gave the scrolls from the Greek libraries to Jacob, an Arab leader of the Hebrews. Alexander's mentor, Aristotle had learned sorcery from Plato, who put everyone in caves craving for knowledge. Plato called it the Cave myth. When Alexander came power, he burned the competition and their houses of knowledge."

Gerwyn peered at the dusty streets from behind some rubble. The Dragons remained submerged in the portal below. They had dressed Gerwyn in some traditional Egyptian garb so that he would not stand out.

"Oh look, there's a camel tied to one of those columns across the way," Gerwyn told them as Ivan began rummaging through the library's collection.

"Look, Elissa, here's a scroll on the evolution of the Pegasus," Ivan said. "Maybe I'll find a drawing of Grandpa."

Elissa peered over Ivan's furry shoulder.

"Oh, the camel sees me! He's freed himself from the column, and he is coming over to visit!" Gerwyn exclaimed, clapping his little hands together in delight. "This is better than finding dragon eggs."

"What?" Ivan exclaimed, putting down the scroll.

Elissa stared at the portal's opening. The camel had allowed Gerwyn to pet his nose before poking his head into the library's dimension.

"Got a lot of scrolls down here," the camel remarked. "Dad mentioned this place to me once. Never thought I'd live to see the day." Gerwyn quieted as he listened to the camel strike a conversation before abruptly changing his mind. "Oh, gotta run. Here comes my rider looking for me," the Camel apologized before he left.

Gerwyn quickly went back inside the portal to the library. In the camel's absence, his attention turned to his surroundings, and he began examining the contents of the library. He studied a drawing of a collapsing tower on the far wall.

"Oh, that's the tower of Babel," Elissa remarked. "Some humans wanted to build an observatory, and the Serpentines zapped them during the intergalactic wars. They became confused and tongue-tied. The trauma created many misunderstandings. One of the human refugees journeyed to Judah and settled there. His name was Abraham. Some of his descendants consulted the star civilization in the Valley of the Indus. They called themselves Brahmins and migrated to the more fertile regions of southern India, where they traded spices with their relatives in Judah. Other descendants joined the celestial warriors from the Cat's Eye and built landing bases in Egypt."

"Look, here's a portrait of my mother in Egypt during the intergalactic wars," Ivan said as he pointed to a catlike figure on papyrus.

"She appears very sleek," Gerwyn observed.

"One of Abraham's descendants was an Egyptian named Moses whom the Serpentines tried to seroconvert," Ivan explained. "They enslaved the entire Egyptian population and conducted experiments on the royal family. After Ramses II freed Egypt from Serpentine control, Moses attempted to give it back. When the Serpentine Federation destroyed most of Lemuria, the North Pole star for the planet switched from Thuban to Polaris. This created many dramatic climate shifts. Moses panicked and fled the city for higher ground. This ceased the Akhenaten revolution, and Moses went to Persia. Later, he realized that he had been duped and remained in exile. Joseph, one of Moses's descendants, made it back to Egypt with an apology and offered the support of twelve tribes."

"When another alien group known as the Black Dogs retook Egypt, Joseph went to prison. During the intergalactic war, the twelve tribes were attacked and scattered," Elissa added. "Joseph led an insurrection from prison and helped restore Egypt to power."

"What is this ice ring around the planet in this picture?" Gerwyn asked.

"The impact of the galactic wars on the planet caused an ice ring to develop that encircled the globe," Ivan replied. "It was like the ring around Saturn, which never recovered from the invasion. It is why people referred to the invader as the Lord of the Rings."

Chapter Four

Put the Golden Rule

To music

And keep it simple

Tune Reference: *Alfie*

----Dionne Warwick

"CAN I GO home now?" Gerwyn whined, tugging on Ivan's fur. "I want my mommy!"

"Ivan, do you think that we scared Gerwyn with the history lesson?" Elissa whispered to Ivan.

Ivan responded in his most masculine voice, "Oh, certainly not. Gerwyn is just hungry."

"No," Gerwyn corrected. "I really just want my mommy. Now!"

"Quick," Ivan urged Elissa in a hushed voice, "humor the little tyke." The three travelers made their way out of the portal and back to the cavern.

"Where's Mommy?" Gerwyn asked in a wee voice as he peered around the empty cave.

"Your parents had to leave on a mission," one of the caretakers explained. He began to brush Elissa's scales. "There has been a tragedy. If it had been just an incident or an accident, then they would not have bothered to leave. Something sad has happened that can't be changed. Please wait for them here."

A tear escaped Gerwyn's eye as he sat on his parents' bed with a sigh. Ivan remained next to Gerwyn while Elissa quietly questioned the caretaker for more details.

"Let's go forage," he told the small boy with a light purr.

The purr lulled Gerwyn. Within minutes he dried his tears. He grabbed a tuft of fur from Ivan's side, and, refusing to let go, he slid off the bed and accompanied Ivan outside the cave.

"Eegan is dead," the caretaker quietly explained to Elissa when he felt certain that he would not be overheard. "They were not expecting Gerwyn to return until late afternoon. They said that it would be a quick trip. His parents left immediately. He was like a brother to Joslin."

"I know," Elissa said softly. "What happened?"

"The Brahmins ambushed Eegan on the Silk Road where he had been trading chocolate for supplies. They seized control of the operation of the Silk Road. A percentage of everything traded must go into their coffers.

"No one was expecting the attack," the caretaker continued. "Pepe has been with the Dragon flyers in Brazil. He is still recovering from a bad injury. Joslin and Yuri hope to find Eegan's adopted son. He's a refugee from the Viking camp. They want to bring him back here. He is the Anglo-Saxon youth who the Vikings captured."

"Oh, do you mean Thor's son, Alfred?" Elissa quizzed. His father was one of the gods that sponsored the star civilization from the red giant star Arcturus.

"The one and the same," the caretaker said. "He has been busy protecting the Noris settlements where Eegan's father, Merilyn, once lived."

As the caretaker and Elissa quietly discussed the latest events, Gerwyn questioned Ivan while they searched for wild edibles. "Hanging out with Sea Dragons instead of Mommy isn't so bad," Ivan began as he sniffed the air for signs of wildlife. "Your grandfather, Arcas, hung out with a mermaid when he was three. They called her Lady of the Lake. She was Merilyn's mother."

"Uh huh," Gerwyn answered, absorbed with picking the berries on a nearby bush.

"Like you, he was smart for his age. By the time he was three, he was a mature male in many ways, spiritually, mentally, and emotionally. Though he was still little, he was the equivalent of a thirteen-year-old."

"What are you getting at?" Gerwyn inquired as he looked up, knowing better than to let a dragon beat around the bush. He held fistfuls of berries in his tiny hands and wrinkled his nose at Ivan.

"Well, maybe you don't need your mommy like you once did," Ivan speculated.

"I was just arriving at the same conclusion myself," Gerwyn agreed with a sigh. Then he smiled brightly. "These berries are very tasty."

"Exactly," Ivan responded.

"I was thinking about going back to the library for more history," Gerwyn remarked. "We could leave my parents a note telling them that we are on an investigation and will be back sometime next week. I noticed a book on Brahmins that had drawings of Eegan's homemade chocolates on it."

"Great idea," Elissa announced as she joined them. She had overheard the last details of the conversation. Approving of any plan that would keep Gerwyn out of harm's way in a useful manner, she nodded silently at Ivan.

Ivan eyed Elissa lustfully as he imagined all the dark places in the library. He winked at Elissa as he thought of spending a week close to her. Elissa noticed the heaviness of his glance and blushed.

Gerwyn ignored them and picked another bunch of berries. "Let's pack up for a week's supply and go." A few short minutes later, Gerwyn and the Sea Dragons returned to the library.

"OK, I'll take this reading room over here to rest. You guys will have to share that reading room. I am tired and I want to go to bed now," the small boy announced as he began laying out his bedroll on the tiled floor.

Elissa's heart leaped for joy when she heard Gerwyn's suggestion. She nudged Ivan toward their reading room.

"Great idea, my little man," Ivan said brightly. He took Elissa's arm in his and offered, "Let me take you to your vacation quarters, my dear."

"Oh, Ivan," Elissa said dreamily, and she grabbed his arm quickly and pushed Ivan onward.

Gerwyn rolled his eyes slightly as he focused on organizing his room. After placing a few cherished objects around his bed, he nestled under the blankets. Then, with a deep breath, he closed his eyes and went to sleep.

When he rose the next day, he sought out the book on Brahmins that he desired. He lifted it from the stack and hauled it to an adjacent table, where he let it drop with a mighty thud. He greedily flipped through the pages to find the pictures that he had seen earlier. Satisfied with the contents, he carefully studied the drawings but skipped the text, which was written in a numeric language.

"Oh, the little man is up," Ivan observed with a yawn. He nudged Elissa softly as she stirred in his arms. "Wake up, my dear. It is back to work."

"Wait until the eggs come," Elissa commented with a smile. "Then we will really have to work."

"Speak for yourself." Ivan grinned.

"I am," she said, snuggling further.

"I found it!" Gerwyn announced, knowing that the dragons could hear him.

"There's our call," Ivan said as he rose. "Time for our next history lesson."

"The Berbers are Dragon flyers from the blue star in Draco," Gerwyn noted. "The Noris come from Centaurus. Philistines are the star civilization from Arcturus, a red giant star. Didn't a little boy named David hit one of their giants with a rock?"

"That's a myth," Ivan corrected as he peered over Gerwyn's shoulder. "The giant was hit in the head with a Serpentine spaceship. Do you think these pock marks on planet Earth are from meteorites?"

"No, there was an electromagnetic blast from a powerful collection of strings like a harp," Gerwyn replied. He pointed to the drawing of a blast that devastated Lemuria. "It came from a star in Dog constellation."

"Earth hasn't been hit by a meteorite since Atlantis sunk," Ivan commented as he studied the drawing. Then a cognitive wave of prescience filled his consciousness, and he dropped the intergalactic subject in favor of life on earth. "That blast killed hundreds and thousands of people. It left sand on what will be one day known as the Oregon coast and produced the Dome of the Rock. They put a piece of that reconstituted rock on the top of every temple across the globe. Ah yes, the Brahmins brought them in. The Brahmins that disagreed with the practice of working with animal gods were hit by the blast as far as the west coast of India. Moses knew it was going to happen ahead of time because they informed him. The surviving Brahmins from India emigrated as far as Ireland. O'Kennedy, the caretaker for Arthur's dragon, comes from a Jewish Brahmin family in India. These people restored trade on the Spice Route after the blast. Celtics such as Fitzgeralds and O'Neills are Atlantean refugees. Later, they partnered with the Lemurian refugees. They call them Druids, you know. The O'Conors are Druid."

"That explains some of our caretakers and flyers," Gerwyn remarked. "When did the Brahmins get infiltrated by the dark side?"

"During the time of the Hebrew insurrection, the royal family rebelled against the invading Serpentines during Solomon's reign. The Brahmins operating the temple brought in a bunch of animal gods too. There were bull and dog gods along with dark Blues and Grays. It was quite a collection."

"Sounds like a mess," Gerwyn said. "I supposed that everyone wanted a piece of the rock."

"It was an obsession with power that grew out of control. The people running the temple wanted more. They spiritually tapped into fallen spirits of the gods. However, they soon discovered that when you start with junk, all you get is junk. After the Brahmins betrayed the Hebrew insurrection to the Serpentines, they eventually decided to tap into the enlightened spirits in parasitic ways. Through rituals and calcified worship, they extended their egos without getting stoned themselves."

Gerwyn blinked and looked up from the book. "Huh?"

"Another story for later," Elissa added as she joined them. "Just remember that not everything on the planet has a soul, unless you happen to be in the MidEarth. As for the rocks, there was a spirit that created the planet. Nothing more. Honor that without getting carried away."

"Sounds like good advice to me," Gerwyn said, having returned his attention to the drawings.

"Me too," a husky, male voice added. A young Anglo Saxon emerged from a portal and into the library.

"Hi, Alfred," Elissa welcomed. "Did you get our note? I see that you are just in time for our history lesson."

"He is going to be great someday," Ivan whispered to Gerwyn, nodding toward Alfred.

Gerwyn looked up from the drawings and studied the young man who was the Thunder god's son. With the help of the Thunder People, the group of Noris who remained celestial, Alfred had held his ego in check. The eastern Noris, called the Hindoos, had taught him emotional balance, whereas the northwestern Noris, known as the Norse, had taught him the wise use of strength.

"I am sorry about Eegan," Gerwyn began.

The Sea Dragons stared in awe at the small boy, who seemed to possess an intuitive grasp of world affairs. Nobody had told him the reason for his parents' departure.

Alfred wiped away a tear that had escaped from his eye. "The traders that became traitors also oppose the *nadas*. They are the ones in northern India that first trapped Eegan in the star sphere. They are in league with the Grays and have ugly, reptilian Dragons. They are over-consumers."

"It is not right to take more than you give. That is the first rule of trading and honoring the spirit that created the planet," Gerwyn said, patting Alfred on the shoulder. His soft words trailed, "Do unto others as..." Alfred lightened at Gerwyn's consoling words. "Isn't that what it is all about?" Gerwyn asked rhetorically.

Alfred began sobbing hysterically. Gerwyn assured him, "Don't worry. They will get their karma."

Chapter Five

Subtleties in life

Come like a

Refreshing wind

To provide vision

For the future

Tune Reference: *(Sittin' On) The Dock Of The Bay*

----Otis Redding

"HEY, PAPA, CAN you throw me some rope from your pouch so that I can tie off a Sea Dragon to this cliff," Alfie shouted to Pepe as he neared the group of Dragon flyers anchored to the face of a vertical rocky exposure. The jungle below them shielded them from being seen by hikers. They could only be viewed by those in the air.

Pepe and his group looked up at Alfie from their encampment in south Connecticut, which would eventually be known as South America. Every Dragon flyer was nesting with his or her Sea Dragon in hammocks tied to the wall of the cliff. Pepe shaded his face and stared between the rays of the sun. He made out the head of a small boy protruding from Elissa's pouch.

"I see that you brought the bambino! Does Joslin know?" Pepe yelled as he tossed Alfie a rope.

"He's a hombre now," Alfie replied, deftly catching the rope and securing Elissa to the cliff.

Alfie reached across a minor abyss and hugged his papa. He noticed that Pepe's face was tear-streaked from grief. Gerwyn remained in Elissa's pouch and waved.

"We left a note," Gerwyn offered.

"Had to take the parents' Sea Dragons out for a spin. They told me to keep an eye on the little man. He is conducting his own investigation." Alfie grinned bravely, but a tear rolled down his cheek. He could remember the first time that he took Pepe's Sea Dragon out for a ride while his parents slept in. Earning the confidence of a Sea Dragon was the only key he needed. All parents knew that if the Sea Dragon consented, then the time had come for the child's first ride.

"They cut short their honeymoon to immediately ride with the other Dragon flyers to the Silk Road," Alfie remarked.

"At least they got two days." Pepe shrugged. "We are in holding pattern here. The base at Pedra Azul is under siege now, and it isn't wise to move forward. So we are waiting for our moment to ambush the supply line."

"Who are you fighting?" Alfie asked. "There are several to choose from these days. Other times it is best to stay out of the fray. When the Brahmins seized control of the Silk Road, they incurred the ire of the *nadas*."

"These are Serpentine," Pepe answered. "There is no getting around these snakes."

"*Ahem*," Ivan interrupted pointedly as he cocked his head toward Gerwyn, who peered wide-eyed out of Elissa's pouch like a baby kangaroo. "Time for our next history lesson, Gerwyn. Take a look around. This is where the intergalactic wars began. The pyramids that Pepe defends were made out of seashells collected thousands of years before the Egyptian ones."

"How did it start?" Gerwyn piped up, his head excitedly bobbing up and down above the edge of Elissa's pouch.

"After they broke into one of the Golden Apples inside the Draco star constellation, the Golden Rule came into existence," Alfie said. "Things changed, but it wasn't our fault. We warned the universe: either respect Paradise or else. That's how the Law of Karma came into existence. It was simply a system of checks and balances, though it was quite a shock for those accustomed to unaccountability."

"Sounds like a good rule to me," Gerwyn reflected.

"Yeah, but that wasn't the rule that proved most powerful," Ivan quipped. "Those Golden Apples were booby-trapped against pretentious intruders. They contained a truth serum that evaporated social masks."

"Oh," Gerwyn replied as he thought more carefully about the subject.

"Which brings us to our beach party," Elissa said, a little embarrassed. "Reduce, reuse, recycle."

"What?" Gerwyn asked, growing more confused.

"After we were done eating the shellfish, we made pyramids out of the shells," Elissa admitted. "You missed it, Ivan."

"I was busy swimming the seven seas," he admitted. Then he winked at her. "How about giving me a guided tour?"

Gerwyn sighed and rolled his eyes slightly. Pepe and Alfie stared perplexedly at the Sea Dragons. Elissa fluttered her scaly, shiny eyes.

The next day, the Sea Dragons flamed their way to the collection of seashell pyramids that Pepe had been guarding.

"Don't tell mom," Gerwyn said to Alfie.

"Don't worry," Alfie assured him. "What happens in South America stays in South America."

Moments later, the group of Dragon flyers landed on top of the largest seashell pyramid.

"Very charming decor, my dear," Ivan complimented Elissa. "Sorta makes you feel like you are still underwater."

"You get the point," Elissa replied with an elegant toss of her golden head. "It makes a Sea Dragon feel right at home. Helps with the metamorphosis from the celestial realm to the planetary one. The sea is like the heavens above. We needed a place to relax and regroup where the veil between the worlds was thinnest. Ninety percent of it is all psychology. The Serpentines couldn't figure out why they drowned once they had been unmasked. They just didn't have what it took to be able to track the heavens during transitions between lives. Eventually, they resorted to vampirism, possession, and genetic manipulation, but that took thousands of years for them to figure out."

Gerwyn began to rub his head.

"Oops, looks like we've said too much again," Elissa quickly added. "Gerwyn looks like he is getting ready to throw up. Here, Ivan, bring him inside for some chocolate. He can play with the little stone animal carvings in the playroom. Alfie, come tell Gerwyn some animal stories."

After some child's play and chocolate, Gerwyn fell asleep on a little bed in the room. Alfie went for a stroll through the corridors in search of more food. Meanwhile, Elissa and Ivan found a secluded room nearby. Pepe and the other Dragon flyers strategized their next move. Alfie joined them after he had found a snack.

"I feel like we are getting nowhere," one of the Dragon flyers remarked.

"Only Elissa and Ivan seem to be getting somewhere," Alfie said ruefully.

"Ah, young love," Pepe sighed.

Gerwyn wandered from his sleeping quarters and joined the conference. "How did the intergalactic wars start?"

"The Serpentines decided to land one of their spacecraft in Brazil," Pepe answered. "It was a blatant violation of all intergalactic agreements. They panicked when they saw their footing on the planet beginning to slip away. All the decaying spirits in the nearby galaxies supported the Serpentines, while the rest fought for Earth's freedom. The planet represented their best interests."

"How did it end?" Gerwyn asked.

"The surviving elves seized the genetic technology of the Serpentines and used it to reproduce. The result was a hauflin," Ivan answered as he sauntered into the conference. With a self-satisfied stretch, he raised his arms in the air and yawned.

"Are there any more hauflins around?" Gerwyn asked.

"No, they eventually mutated to the human form to avoid detection by the Serpentines and other foes from the intergalactic wars," Ivan said as he looked directly at Gerwyn with his languid, tiger-like eyes. "They mingled with star civilizations all over the planet. Most of the world's pyramids had portals to the MidEarth. They have all been sealed except for the seven in South America."

"Can we go visit one?" Gerwyn asked.

"When Elissa's caretaker finishes cleaning her scales," Ivan replied.

"OK, I'll get the packs ready," Alfie announced. "Maybe the hauflins have some ideas on how to elude the Grays that are trying to retake this base for their spaceships."

"I thought you said that there were no more hauflins around," Gerwyn reminded Alfie.

"There aren't any around here for the Serpentines to find," Alfie insisted. "You have to go into the MidEarth to find a hauflin. There's a remaining delegation there. Their job is to continue the cultivation of the earth's spirit, known as Gaia."

Moment later, Elissa, Ivan, Alfie, and Gerwyn left the pyramid through a secret passageway and headed into the heart of the nearby jungle. Elissa led the way, and Ivan followed behind the humans. Occasionally the Sea Dragon pounced, cat-like, on small prey hiding in the underbrush. He tossed some of his prizes to Elissa for her to eat along the way. Alfie and Gerwyn ignored the munching Sea Dragons and contented themselves with a few berries.

"Here it is," Elissa announced as she cleared some brush away from a wooden raft and then headed for the Amazon River ten yards away. After placing the raft in the water, she announced, "All on board. Ivan and I will push the raft from the water."

Gerwyn and Alfie sat down in the raft as the Sea Dragons waded into the water. The sun appeared in the opening over the water and warmed them with its golden rays that glistened off the river's misty reflection. Both humans fell into a deep sleep soon after the raft left the riverbank.

Chapter Six

Never turn your back

On yesterday

Tune Reference: *Right Back Where We Started From*

----Maxine Nightingale

WHEN GEREWYN AND Alfie awoke, they discovered that they were out of the jungle. The terrain had changed to a scene reminiscent of an old English countryside with bogs, small farms, and cottages. Alfie stretched his long, muscular arms as Elissa and Ivan delightedly bobbed in the free-flowing river. Gerwyn placed one hand on Alfie's shoulder and rose up on his small legs. He used Alfie to steady himself while he peered at the new surroundings. He had never seen an English countryside with fairies, elves, and hauflins.

"Alfie, Alfie!" Gerwyn exclaimed, trembling with excitement. "These people are little like me!"

Alfie laughed. "You should get along just fine."

The Sea Dragons pushed the drifting raft toward an embankment so that Gerwyn and Alfie could disembark. A throng of hauflinss waited for them on the dock. They greeted the newcomers as they stepped onto the dock.

"Welcome to the MidEarth. I am Leo, the mayor of this hauflin community," he said as he shook Alfie's hand. Then Leo lowered his head to look at Gerwyn, who stood four inches smaller than him. "They told us that you were coming."

"Who are 'they'?" Alfie queried.

"Gerwyn's mother, Queen Joslin," Mayor Leo answered, and he quickly ushered Gerwyn off the dock before the distracted lad fell off.

A hauflin lifted Gerwyn to his shoulders, and they headed into town with the crowd. Alfie remained behind with Mayor Leo. Staring wide-eyed, Gerwyn and the hauflins seemed enchanted with the stature of each other.

"How did the queen know?" Alfie questioned.

"She married a man who has the eye of a tiger," Mayor Leo quipped as Ivan emerged from the water, clearing his throat. Mayor Leo briefly glanced in Ivan's direction before adding, "She maintains communications with the pyramid bases and MidEarth through the old Horsetail network. She didn't want her toddler to wander too far."

"Oh," Alfie responded, still perplexed. "What is the Horsetail network?"

"You mean Equisetum?" Mayor Leo asked in disbelief. "How could you miss the important lesson on this an ancient self-assembling semiconductor system that used for communication by the plant kingdom? The Horsetail plants put it in place after the land cooled sufficiently for habitation. Didn't your teachers mention it?"

"Oh," Alfie repeated, scratching his head and imagining the possibilities of using the Horsetail network to kick the Vikings out of London again.

"Looks like the pressure to find dragon eggs has dissipated," Ivan whispered to Elissa. "The little man has found playmates his own size."

The golden Sea Dragon queen swiftly nudged Ivan in the ribs before gracefully accepting the elves' offer to clean her scales. Ivan gasped slightly with the blow. He winked at Elissa while caretakers began grooming his soft brown fur.

Meanwhile, the group of hauflins carried Gerwyn through the town square and took him to a cottage on the far side of town. One of the hauflins knocked on the heavy wood door, and a middle-aged hauflin answered it. He peered at the crowd and the small boy. When he saw the Sea Dragons being groomed by caretakers on the nearby hillside, he smiled.

"C'mon in," he told Gerwyn. "You must be Prince Gerwyn. I heard that you were coming. My name is Bilbo. Please join me by the hearth for a cup of tea."

The hauflin who had been carrying Gerwyn lowered him to the ground, and the toddler raced into the cottage. At Bilbo's invitation, he sat down in a comfortable chair by the fire. Bilbo waved the crowd away and invited Gerwyn to partake of an assortment of pastries, cheese, and soup. Despite his ravenous hunger, Gerwyn remained gracefully polite and did not partake. Instead, the small boy assumed a businesslike air and abruptly began their discussion.

"How did you win the intergalactic wars?" he asked Bilbo, as he respectfully munched on a piece of cheese.

"Well, it took a while for us to figure out how to do it," Bilbo began. "There were seven rings in the beginning. Each ring represented the energetic input of the seven different celestial races that met on Eltanin, the blue star in the ancient Greek constellation known as Draco."

Gerwyn nodded his understanding, but another thought crossed his mind. "Ivan told me that Eltanin was a red giant star."

"It was," Bilbo answered. "Until it collapsed under the strain of those who the Greeks call gods and goddesses now. Only Diana survived, but that is another story."

"Each celestial group took a twenty-four-hour period to make their ring. This is why they say that the planet was made in seven days. They determined the time from calculations describing the rotation of the planet in the galaxy around the Sun star, which served as the energy source for the solar system. Jupiter, as you know it, was one of the prototypes for Earth. They scrapped the project when one of the former celestials became lost in his ego. Instead of bringing the energy down in a concrete and practical manner, Zeus dallied and never manifested the higher frequencies that are required to sustain life. He and his collection of revolutionaries remained as a gas in the sky, while being worshipped as calcified icons by the star civilizations that he tormented with his diversions."

"Oh." Gerwyn nodded before reaching for a spoon and a mug of hot soup. Suddenly eager for Bilbo to get on with the story, he began eating heartily.

Bilbo smiled as the young boy succumbed to his appetite. His ploy had worked. Now that his guest had finally relaxed, he hurried to the point of the story. "Simply stated," he said, looking directly into Gerwyn's eyes, "we gave fake rings to the various pharaohs and Turks while we destroyed all the real rings one by one. Through the ages, we infused their energy into the crystalline matrix of the planet, similar to the Equisetum networks."

"Got it," Gerwyn said. "That's how Mom keeps up with me."

Bilbo laughed. "Yes, you are correct. The Horsetail network follows the crystalline matrix from the Noris. Their ring symbolized the energy of 'becoming.'"

"They must be very philosophical," Gerwyn observed.

Bilbo smiled with a nod. "Yes, they are. The Noris contributed the energy of organized thought."

Gerwyn's eyes began to droop as his stomach filled. Bilbo noticed that he had arrived at the end of their discussion. He encouraged Gerwyn to climb into a loft bed at the other end of the room. Gerwyn obeyed, and soon lapsed into a contented sleep.

The next day, he arose and scurried down the ladder to find Bilbo. He observed Alfie snoozing in the bed below his. Without awaking his friend, Gerwyn searched for signs of his host in the cottage. Bilbo had left a bowl of oatmeal warming on the woodstove for his guests. Gerwyn grabbed a bowl and measured out some oatmeal before sitting down at a nearby table. The small table stood under a window and Gerwyn surveyed the countryside as he ate his breakfast. He spied Bilbo in the distance, walking along the river's edge. Gerwyn quickly finished his bowl of oatmeal and hurried outside to catch up with Bilbo. However, his host seemed to have disappeared in the countryside.

"Are you ready to go back?" Elissa hollered.

Gerwyn watched the two Sea Dragons frolicking in the river. Their beautiful, shiny scales and fur glistened in the spray of the droplets surrounding them. He thought about what Bilbo had told him the previous night. "Yes, I think I am done here. Shouldn't I say good-bye to Bilbo first?"

"Don't worry about Bilbo," Ivan answered, hugging Elissa. "He prefers to be a man of few words for the moment. He told us that he likes your style. He wants you to come back and visit again soon. He had to leave for important business in the next shire. Did he answer your question?"

Gerwyn eagerly nodded his head in delight. "Yes, and he told me even more than what I wanted to know."

"Well, there we have it," Elissa acknowledged. "Enough said."

Moments later, Alfie emerged from the cottage with a map in his hands. "Bilbo told me about another portal system that we could take to avoid the skirmishes along the Amazon." The tall, muscular man gazed thoughtfully into the distance. "It is just over the hill."

Chapter Seven

The lively art
Of being discriminate

Tune Reference: *Because Of You*
----Kelly Clarkson

"ALL ROADS LEAD to Mama," Gerwyn observed with delight as he sauntered over the hill.

In the valley below, he could see the familiar sapphire blue of Lake Hovsgol. He motioned to the Sea Dragons to fly him and Alfie back to the cave where his parents had started their honeymoon. As he surveyed the familiar terrain below, he reflected on what he had learned. He asked Elissa, "Where did the Turks come from?"

"They were refugees from another galaxy called Andromeda," Elissa answered. "They were a collection of artisans that were known for their craftsmanship. The Serpentines blew up their base, leaving behind dark matter. The star civilizations from Pleiades and Orion helped a few escape. They came long before the Lemurians fled Mu. They eventually partnered with the human family in building Babylon, where they taught them various crafts. When it was attacked, they decided to split off from Abraham's group as a diversion. Through the years, they disappeared into the security of the MidEarth, only to reappear centuries later when it was safe. Historically, the

Turks are difficult to pin down. Unfortunately, right now the Grays have gotten the best of them, but the Sufis are attempting to restore spiritual order."

Gerwyn stared into space as they closed in on the familiar cave. The additional information felt overwhelming. He admitted, "I am ready to go home now."

"There's my baby!" Joslin yelled as they landed at the entrance of the cave. She rushed to scoop Gerwyn into her arms. Glancing sideways at Alfie, she added, "How did it go?"

Alfie grinned. "He learned a lot."

Joslin lowered Gerwyn to the ground before Yuri lifted him to his shoulders. She collected Gerwyn's things from Elissa and showed them to Yuri. Yuri nodded as she produced a tiny metal box from Elissa's pouch.

"Gerwyn, where did you get this ring?" she asked, raising a large turquoise ring from the box.

"Oh, that is something Bilbo asked me to give to you," Gerwyn explained. "He left it for me at breakfast with your name on it. He told me about it the night before, but I fell asleep. He said to give you the Ring of Beauty. He said that you would know what to do with it."

"Oh, OK, I suppose that I'll figure it out." Joslin sighed as she examined the Ring of Beauty curiously. "The contribution of the Regulus star system to the creation of this planet was beauty."

Yuri softly patted Gerwyn on the back and quietly posed a question to his wife: "How many more rings are left?"

"None," Joslin answered. "This one is a fake. It is to be used as a decoy. It's a long story. Let's get Gerwyn settled. I want him to tell me about all his big adventures."

"Only if you tell me more about the Seven Rings," he insisted.

"Oh, my little man," Alfie commented as he handed the Sea Dragons over to caretakers, "you drive a hard bargain."

"It is called the grand illusion," Joslin remarked as she led the group toward the kitchen for refreshments.

"So tell us more about the Seven Rings," Yuri began, placing Gerwyn beside him on a bench.

Joslin handed him a cup of tea and sat down on a bench across from them. Alfie sat down next to Joslin. Gerwyn helped himself to a cup of warm soup from a pot left on the table.

"I only know what my father, King Arcas, told me as we walked along the beach one day," she said. "The Pleiades forged a Ring of Power, which was the strongest ring of the seven. It contained nuclear energy and proved even more powerful than the Ring of Love, which the celestials from Orion had made."

Joslin looked at the group gathered around her at the table. She paused briefly for their responses. Alfie picked up the discussion.

"When I visited Red Deer with Eegan last year, I met the Native Americans at Shambala's new location. Eegan told me that the Native Americans consist of two star civilizations. One came from the blue giant Spica and the other group was from Pleiades. Those from Pleiades inhabited the southwest and continued where their ancestors, the Anasazi, had left off."

"I want to see Red Deer, where Eegan relocated Shambala," Gerwyn piped in, looking up from his soup for his parents' approval.

"Maybe we can catch the Dance of the Masks," Alfie suggested, glancing quickly at Queen Joslin for her reaction.

Out of the corner of his eye, he noticed Joslin winking at Yuri, and he smiled, knowing that the couple wished to resume their honeymoon. Yuri reached under the table for Joslin's hand. Gerwyn scarcely noticed. Instead, he bounced up and down exuberantly after his mother and father silently nodded their approval.

"Great! I'll start packing!" Gerwyn shouted with enthusiasm.

"Wait a moment, young man!" his mother demanded. "Finish eating first." Gerwyn complied.

"So, Gerwyn, what do you know about Native Americans?" his father quizzed.

"Nothing," he replied confidently as he hurriedly finished his soup.

"Just what I thought," his father said ruefully. "Now listen carefully. Stay away from the Native Americans who have merged with the Grays. They are no longer Gray. They are Red Skins. They haven't forgotten their barbaric, warlike ways. They trade human scalps like they are bars of chocolate from South America."

Gerwyn gulped and almost dropped his spoon in his bowl. Alfie looked at him sternly and nodded his agreement with Yuri. Joslin shrugged.

"Not all of the colored Grays made the conversion," she explained. "Some are still struggling."

Gerwyn sighed as he leaned his head over his raised arm. Realizing that he needed more historical information, he asked, "What was the contribution of the star civilization from Spica?"

"Lucidity," Joslin answered. "You need it to see the light of truth."

"It is like the Raven Dance," Alfie interjected. "In the story, the raven is the hero who brings light to the world so that the people can see how beautiful it is."

"The star civilization from Spica wished to avoid the problem associated with egos and gods, so they presented the earth spirits with god status," Joslin explained. "Like the tricky raven, they outsmarted the Serpentines who had influenced those celestials immobilized by their own egos."

"That is why Shambala is safe at Red Deer," Alfie added with a wry grin. "Like their heroes, raven and coyote, they are tricksters. They know how to play the dark to see the light. Nothing more. Nothing less."

Gerwyn laughed and clapped his hands together in delight. Then he pointed at the turquoise ring that Bilbo had given to Joslin. Joslin exposed the ring in the palm of her hand as he commented, "It all is very tricky. No wonder they brought the gift of lucidity to the new planet."

Chapter Eight

Some things in life

Never die

Or give up

Tune Reference: *Bang A Gong (Get It On)*

----T. Rex

TWO WEEKS LATER, Gerwyn and Alfie returned from Red Deer. Gerwyn sported a coyote mask, and he wore it at the table. While everyone else met in the cavern, Elissa and Ivan decided to take a walk together.

"So they put you in the Raven Dance," Joslin observed. She stared at her masked son sitting across from her.

Without a word, Gerwyn nodded the mask affirmatively. Alfie retrieved a raven mask from his gear bag and covered his face. He said, "They made one for me too. I danced the mask on our last night. The Norse revered raven, who symbolizes 'thought' and 'memory' during life passages. He cloaks the souls in womb-like darkness so that they can rebirth themselves. This was very important during the intergalactic wars."

Gerwyn pulled on his father's tunic and asked, "May I go visit the star civilization from the Sun next? They told us about the Sons of Heaven in China, Japan, and Vietnam."

"When you go, stay away from the Grays that settled there," Yuri remarked.

"They have yellow skin," Alfie rejoined, removing his raven mask.

"That shouldn't be hard to miss," Gerwyn said as he removed the coyote mask and looked around. "Where did those dragons go?"

"They are getting it on," Alfie answered.

"Let's go. I'm ready to go meet the Sons of Heaven," Gerwyn announced impatiently. With a little clap, he said, "Let's get it on."

"Just a minute, young man. Not so fast," Joslin reprimanded him. "Before you pay a respectful visit to any star civilization in a region full of dangers, you need to know a little bit more about where they are coming from."

Yuri nodded at Gerwyn for parental emphasis. "She is right, you know."

Alfie nodded with a wry smile. "I wouldn't want you coming around my place if you didn't have a clue about me."

Gerwyn stopped in his tracks, pondering the situation for a few moments. "OK, I get it," he admitted. "What is the ring of the Sun star civilization?"

"Take a lucky guess," his mother encouraged him.

Yuri winked at his son, who was carefully studying his mother as he considered her words. After a few seconds, he slowly began, "It is luck."

"Yes, you hear me well," Joslin softly replied. She added, "The Ring of Luck came from the Sun star civilization. Now go find those frolicking Sea Dragons, and I'll see you back here in two weeks!"

"C'mon, Alfie. Now is our chance," Gerwyn said enthusiastically as he put his coyote mask aside and went to repack his gear. "Maybe we'll find some dragon eggs."

Alfie chuckled. "From the mouth of babes."

"He hasn't yet put it all together," Yuri observed.

"That's OK," Joslin confessed. "It helps keep him out of trouble. Here, Alfie, you take this fake Ring of Beauty as a precaution. They never harm those who carry the rings. They are afraid they might lose something. If they press you for it, throw it in a volcano or in the ocean. That will keep them searching for a while. These fake rings melt quickly and rust beyond recognition in a matter of minutes."

Alfie took the fake Ring of Beauty and eyed it curiously. "The things we have to do these days."

"It is called 'fighting like the devil,'" Yuri informed him. "Just remember to have fun."

"Wait until young Gerwyn figures out where dragon eggs come from." He laughed. "There will be no stopping us then."

"By then, he will have learned manners," Yuri added.

Alfie watched the two Sea Dragons enter the room arm in arm as he agreed, "You're right. And that is a good thing."

"Gerwyn told us that it was time to get it on in China," Ivan said with a nod to his partner.

Elissa blushed slightly. Her golden scales glittered in the candlelight of the cave. She sighed. "Oh, Ivan, Asia is so much fun in autumn."

"I hear they have some great tantric positions there," he answered with a wink.

Elissa's scales burned brightly at Ivan's insinuation.

Alfie rose from his seat and left the room to prepare for the next excursion. "Start packing. We leave in two hours."

Yuri and Joslin looked at each other for a few moments. Joslin remained seated and rested her head on one arm. "He is growing up so quick."

"I know," Yuri answered. "What ring did the star civilization from Arcturus bring?"

"Ring of Determination," Joslin answered. "They needed it after a Serpentine starship took out one of their leaders from Arcturus. I think they called him Goliath. Later they teamed up with Solomon to help build a temple. The temple self-destructed when they started fighting over it with other sons of Abraham. They were alarmed about losing their power base."

"I suppose that a temple is a little bit more difficult to destroy than a ring," Yuri commented.

"Yes, the power base has diminished through the years, but the Serpentines keep trying to get someone else to restore it for them. They are parasites, the quintessential energy vampire," Joslin remarked. "The creative spirit of the rings increased once they were destroyed. People came to embody their energy, and it multiplied through the ages."

"Tell me about the ring from Centaurus," he asked. "I want to stay one step ahead of my son."

"Alfie could probably answer that better than me," Joslin admitted. "He is Noris, which are from the Centaurus galaxy. The Centaurus people fled the Serpentine attack so quickly that the dust still remains in orbit. They contributed the Ring of Ascendance."

"It is always great to have a way out, especially if you are in a hurry," Yuri surmised.

"Over time it has become less dramatic and more metaphorical," Joslin commented. "The Serpentines found this ring and sabotaged it. As a result, some of the Noris Vikings teamed up with the Grays. They hoped that their technological knowledge might save them some trouble. But, as you know, there are truly no shortcuts. They call them Whites."

"Let me guess," Yuri began. "Those refugees who partnered with the Grays in Africa were known as Blacks."

"Great!" Joslin applauded in earnest. "You are figuring it out. Now you are three steps ahead of Gerwyn."

"It was only a matter of time," he told her.

"You are catching on," she observed.

Chapter Nine

The lively art of

Being unreasonable

Tune Reference: *Whatever It Takes*

----Lifehouse

JOSLIN LOOKED AWAY from Yuri as she finished her last sentence.

"I'm loosing you," Yuri said as he reached for her hands. He noticed the tears in her eyes.

"It is a story that is difficult to tell," she confessed. "Gerwyn is forcing me to confront the past in his innocent adventures."

"I can sense that," Yuri said. "You seem to be the only one who knows these details."

"My parents died such terrible deaths," she remarked. "I haven't recovered from the shock of Eegan's passing. Bilbo knows. That is why he gave the fake ring to Gerwyn to bring to me. Bilbo not only wants me to step up protection, but he wants me to recall our history too."

"I'm listening," Yuri said encouragingly. "If you don't want Gerwyn to go to Asia, just say so."

"No, it is not Gerwyn," Joslin admitted. "Somehow I feel that he is safer in the wanderings of his own invention than being here. I must come to grips with the reality of the changing situation."

"What troubles me is that the details of Eegan's death remain obscure," Yuri confessed. "He apparently was killed in a dispute. He was on to something."

"Or on something." Joslin sighed as a tear escaped her eye. "They hooked him and this means that those from Aldebaran control the Silk Road now."

"It is a new enemy on planet Earth," Yuri observed.

"Yes, I suspect Eegan's betrayal," Joslin replied. "Our enemies have learned how to adapt to the human form and walk among the Brahmins undetected."

"Well, I suppose he did the world a favor by smoking them out," Yuri commented, speaking the truth, even if it brought more tears to Joslin's eyes.

"My father warned me about those from Aldebaran," Joslin reflected. "They seduced many celestials into becoming gods and goddesses to the point that they forgot what it was like to live and become human. They keep them in constant pain."

"Tell me more about what happened to your father," Yuri requested, changing the subject slightly.

"His enemies tortured him to death," Joslin explained. "The Serpentines wanted to destroy his soul. Whatever they cannot possess, they anihilate. It tidies the world for them."

"What happened to the Ring of Ascendance?" Yuri quizzed, trying to understand the real meaning of Joslin's grief.

"My father told me that during the intergalactic wars, those from Aldebaran stole the ring from Alfie's grandfather, Odin," Joslin explained, drying her tears with Yuri's logical approach.

"That's why all the other rings were destroyed?" Yuri speculated.

Joslin shook her head. "There is more to the story. Those from Aldebaran razed the civilization on Pleiades, after the Serpentines attacked their star base. The surviving souls could be tracked via their celestial wounds. They would have been gone to oblivion if they had tried to ascend. My father learned how to transcend pain, though I suspect that Eegan took the easy way out. My father told me that I needed to heal to avoid being tracked myself."

"What our about our son?" Yuri questioned.

"He is a soul from Cassiopeia," Joslin answered, her countenance communicating her relief. "They protected the celestial realm around Draco. They appear immune from the Serpentines and invaders from Aldebaran. Only the Grays forced them to seek refuge elsewhere."

"When Gerwyn takes off, let's go back to the Silk Road," Yuri proposed. "There may be some more clues that we missed."

Joslin nodded, and then she hugged Yuri as she sobbed softly in his arms. After they waved Gerwyn off, they headed for the Silk Road through a portal. When they arrived at the site where Eegan had last been seen alive, they studied the uninhabited terrain. A recent windstorm had swept the area clear.

"Life in the desert," Joslin quipped. "Nothing lingers."

"I know," Yuri replied ruefully as he knelt over on object half-buried in the dirt and brushed away the sand. He stood up after retrieving the object. "Do you think Eegan left his ring for us to find?"

"Best ring I've seen in a while," Joslin remarked, brushing away a tear as she walked toward Yuri for a closer look. "He wanted us to come back, otherwise he would have taken his ring with him."

"He left a note inside the chamber," Yuri remarked. Before opening it, Yuri looked around uneasily. "Let's get out of here first. That dust cloud over the far hill means that a group of marauders are racing toward us on horseback. They know that we are here."

"It is the *nadas*, the Eye-in-the-Sky gang," Joslin sensed. "Back to the portal, quick."

Moments later, Joslin and Yuri sat at the table in the cave and opened the ring's chamber. A small hex wrench dropped from the ring and landed on the wood table along with a tiny folded note. Yuri studied the hex wrench carefully as Joslin seized the note and began unfolding it.

"This is the key to your father. Love, Eegan," Joslin read. "I didn't know that my father had a key. Eegan knew that I would be the one reading the note in the ring's chamber."

"Don't you just love when you are set up?" Yuri said with a sideways glance. Then he returned his attention to the hex wrench. "It's too delicate for a chastity belt."

"Leave it to Dad to have a sense of humor during a dark time like this." Joslin sighed as she turned around on the bench and stared into space. "That is how he kept everyone focused. He'd use his dry wit to chase away their fears. The grimmer the situation, the drier he became. He also became more cryptic. People were too busy trying to figure him out to be scared." She paused as she lifted both hands and rubbed her head. "This means that we should really be scared."

"Oh," Yuri said abruptly as the meaning of the note began to sink into his consciousness. "What do we do now?"

"Keep thinking, of course," Joslin instructed.

"Oh," Yuri repeated in the same abrupt tone.

"Eegan is correct in saying this is the key to my father," Joslin commented as she reviewed the scenes in her mind. "Though, I am not sure that the message is all metaphorical. Dad had a way of being cryptic that eluded his enemies. Only those that had loving intentions could understand his meaning. It also served the purpose of using the imagination to bring out the depth of the message on many dimensions, like a story inside a story inside a story that goes on forever."

"That's the key…," Yuri mused. "He does seem to go on forever, though he is not immortal. He does it a different way than a god or vampire. It is much less draining, more empowering."

"I know," Joslin said, lowering her shoulders with a deep breath. "This means that forever must be threatened with Eegan's passing."

"The next question is why does Eegan's passing threaten our future?" Yuri asked. "Maybe it has more to do with those who killed him? Do you think his attackers thought they killed a harmless wizened man hawking chocolate or do you think they purposely killed Eegan, the powerful Druid?"

"I don't know," Joslin answered. "Regardless, the message is a warning waiting to be validated. We must take heed."

"Wait. You just quit thinking," Yuri accused her with a smile. "Here, let me do it for you."

Joslin almost laughed as her eyes flashed at the man she loved.

Noting that he had her full and careful attention, Yuri continued, "The Eye-in-the-Sky gang watches us, but they came to attack on horses. Tell me what that means."

"The Brahmins and *nadas* oppose each other now," Joslin said. "Rome wants to put a picture of the Eye-in-the-Sky on the back of their money, which the Brahmins use in their trades with the *nadas*."

Yuri listened to her answer thoughtfully. "Now we are getting somewhere."

Joslin cocked her head to the side with a grin. Yuri saw a thought cross her mind and laughed at his revelation. His lover had reminded him of their primary mission in the cave without speaking.

"This is getting scary," he said with an air of wonder.

Joslin burst out laughing. Unable to contain his own mirth, he kissed her forehead. She responded by planting a soft, direct kiss on his lips.

Chapter Ten

Hope comes with healthy risks

As well as sweet surrender

Tune Reference: *Only Hope*

----Switchfoot

JOSLIN LINGERED IN Yuri's arms the next morning and daydreamed about finding the lock that matched the hex wrench key. She lazily watched the brilliant streaks of sunlight reflect off the walls of the cave. Yuri's eyes flicker in the dawn light as he pulled her closer in his semiconscious state.

"Do you have it all figured out?" he asked softly in a deep, sleepy voice.

The directness of his words woke her from her daydream. She nestled into his embrace and responded, "Yes."

"I thought so," he stated, closing his eyes. "I could see the look on your face. Where are we going next?"

"The Library in Rhakotis," she murmured.

"That will be easy," he agreed. "We can take the portal."

Several hours later, Yuri and Joslin were combing through books in the Technology section.

"Here it is," Joslin said as she compared the hex wrench key to a picture in the book. "Dad did most of the electronics for the machines in the

Avebury shataquah before the move to Stonehenge. It looks as if this key fits this device."

Yuri peered over her shoulder at the device in the picture and studied the insertion point of the key. "That is it all right. The key activates a nuclear containment shield. Not to panic, but we are onto big stuff."

Joslin looked up from the book and nodded silently at him. "It is a clue leading to more clues. Looks like it is time to activate the nuclear protection shield," she remarked. "Let's not procrastinate."

"I agree," Yuri replied as he hurriedly put the books away and collected their things. "There is a portal from the Rhakotis Library to the Electronics lab at Stonehenge. Let's go."

Joslin and Yuri entered the portal and reached an empty Electronics lab.

"No one is here," Joslin observed.

"That is because the Electronics lab now exists in another dimension," Yuri answered, examining his surroundings with all his catlike senses. "We are covered by a thick cloud of dark smoke."

"Oh, that's not good," Joslin announced as she searched the room for the device that matched the hex wrench key. She quickly spotted it in a corner away from the other machines in the room. Placing the key in the indicated hole, she swiftly rotated it a quarter turn until it stopped. A larger, golden hex key wrench dropped from a drawer in the machine. A note written in gold letters on papyrus covered half of the key. Joslin picked up the key and note and read it out loud to Yuri, who continued to study the contents of the room. "Sure enough. It is another clue. Dad was on a roll. It reads, 'Follow the Yellow Silk Road.'"

"We'll have to go back to the Rhakotis Library for that portal," Yuri told her.

"I was just beginning to think that there was no place like home. Time to go," Joslin said as she tucked the key and note away in a pocket inside her lightweight, invisible armor.

Yuri and Joslin left the portal from the Rhakotis Library for the Silk Road in China. The portal dropped them off at Chang'an, which translated to Perpetual Peace. Yuri and Joslin strolled through the city, looking for another clue that matched their golden hex key.

"Maybe we'll see our son here," Yuri remarked as he nodded wide-eyed at Joslin.

"Just look for a small Caucasian with two large Sea Dragons," Joslin quipped.

Yuri chuckled as he imagined the sight of Gerwyn with his entourage. Suddenly, from out of the shadows, a hooded figure approached Joslin, who had disguised herself with the attire of a male Silk Road trader. Yuri stepped toward his wife to protect her but gasped when the hooded figure exposed part of her face. "Kuan Yin!"

Without creating a scene, Kuan Yin ushered Yuri and Joslin into a private tent. Joslin warmly embraced the goddess as Yuri sighed with relief. Kuan Yin extended her arms to include Yuri and patted him on the back.

"Great job, you two. I see that you found the golden hex key." She smiled with a few tears in her eyes. "Eegan's message got through."

"I'll say," Joslin answered. "Our honeymoon has turned into an odyssey."

"They told me." She sighed. "I warned Eegan to avoid the Spice Route, but he never paid attention to me."

"Some have more problems than others," Joslin consoled her. "I'm not happy about it either. He let his fetish get the better of him."

"Well, at least he retained enough wit to get you your father's key," Kuan Yin muttered.

"It's another history lesson," Yuri admitted.

"Oh, there is more to come," she promised. "That is what you get with these save-the-world projects. The past is the key to the future."

Yuri threw his hands in the air. "Well, let's go back."

"Mommy, Daddy!" a small voice exclaimed. Gerwyn came racing inside the tent and almost knocked Joslin over with his embrace.

"Well, what have we here?" Kuan Yin laughed. "It's a family reunion."

"I was just wondering if we'd find each other here," Yuri said as he scooped his small son into his arms with a light kiss.

"Mommy, Daddy, you must come and meet the Sons of Heaven," Gerwyn insisted. "They told me that I could find you here with Kuan Yin in this tent. They sensed your coming."

"I think this golden hex key announces itself," Joslin commented. Then she turned to Kuan Yin. "Please introduce us to your family."

"First we must find the match for the golden key. It is important," she replied.

Joslin approached Gerwyn, who was sitting on Yuri's shoulders. She showed him the golden hex key. "Gerwyn, have you seen where this belongs?"

"Oh yes." He eagerly nodded. "It opens one of the palace gates."

Kuan Yin winked at Joslin. "There's no time to waste. My relatives can direct us to that gate. They showed Gerwyn around earlier this afternoon. What synchronicity!"

The group resumed their various disguises and made their way past the tents of the city toward the palace. The guards recognized Kuan Yin as soon as she dropped her hood. An attendant sounded a bugle, and moments later the emperor emerged to escort them.

"Gerwyn's gate is over on the north side," he told them with a knowing wink. "I sensed that it would be important today."

Joslin inserted the golden hex key in the lock. A small box near the gate hummed before it automatically opened. They hurriedly went inside the grounds.

"They call it a nuclear reactor," Yuri explained, standing in front of a column with an opening at the top.

"Why here?" Joslin asked.

"Your father built it," the emperor said. "In a past life, he served as the Turkish wizard who possessed the Ring of Power."

"Oh, I see," Joslin said. "Sort of."

Kuan Yin interjected, "The Ring of Power contained the transmuted energy of the Pleiades destruction."

"Oh." Joslin shuddered at the thought of the Serpentine attack on Pleiades two hundred and fifty-million years ago.

"In that past life, your father barely escaped the attack on the Pleiades," Kuan Yin explained. "Choosing to become empowered by the experience, your father gifted planet Earth with the Ring of Power. This ensured the new planet's survival. During the intergalactic wars, he destroyed the ring and placed some of the energy in this particular nuclear reactor."

"So there is hope," Yuri remarked, cradling his son in his arms.

"You're looking at 'im." Joslin smiled.

"We always have each other," Kuan Yin remarked with a philosophical air.

61

Chapter Eleven

Nothing is ever lost

Through the eyes of a child

And the unschooled

Tune Reference: *Wonderful World*

----Sam Cooke

"LOOK, MOMMY AND Daddy, there's a beautiful yellow Feathered Dragon guarding the nuclear reactor!" Gerwyn exclaimed, pointing toward an elegant creature emerging from the shadows behind the gate.

"It's Freddie the Feathered Dragon," the emperor said. "He is a loaner from the Yucatan Peninsula."

Freddie breathed an impressive ring of fire before he met the group gathered at the gate. He recognized the emperor, who introduced Queen Joslin as the daughter of King Arcas.

Freddie's eyes twinkled at the memory, and he regally nodded his feathered crown at her family.

"Oh yes, Eegan finally got the ring to you. It took him long enough. I have been waiting for you," he told them. "Come with me."

Alfie ran past the emperor and stood beside Yuri. "I'm coming too. The Sea Dragons are getting prepared for the next trip."

"Mommy and Daddy, I am going to visit the Yucatan Peninsula next. I really like the color on the Feathered Dragons," Gerwyn told her.

"We'll talk about it afterward," Joslin insisted as she followed Freddie. "Let's see what is going on here first."

Kuan Yin asked the emperor to stay behind and have the guards bring the Sea Dragons over to watch the gate, and then she hurried after Joslin and the rest. Freddie led them to a cylindrical smokestack made of bricks. He removed a fruity-red pyramidal crystal from a shelf in the wall and handed it to Joslin. There was another papyrus note that came with the crystal. Joslin unfolded the note and skimmed through it.

"You get your wish. The next stop is the Yucatan Peninsula, where guardians watch the Chicxulub crater in the Caribbean basin," Joslin told Gerwyn.

"What are they watching?" Gerwyn questioned.

"It is the region where the largest Atlantean crystal sank," Yuri explained to Gerwyn. "It still emits enough electromagnetic energy to rearrange the magnetic dipoles in the human occiput, though it is decaying."

"Oh, people easily get lost in the area, and the birdlike dragons rescue them," Gerwyn observed.

"You got it," Joslin answered. "This pyramidal red crystal contains the amount of radiation needed to counteract the stray frequencies at the sunken Atlantean crystal site. We will be able to navigate the area without getting lost."

Appearing perplexed, Joslin shook her head over the note before Kuan Yin interceded. "What the note didn't tell you was the reason you must navigate the area."

"Yes, I know," Joslin said slowly. "That is the problem. Perhaps you can elucidate the matter?"

"The Grays are trying to resurrect the Atlantean crystal," Kuan Yin said. "That is just one of the emergencies."

"Oh," Joslin replied. "We need to regroup now." Then she took a deep breath and decided. "Let's spend the night here. Things are getting complicated quickly and I need to learn more about this reactor."

"I can explain," Alfie offered. "I learned about nuclear fusion reactions from the Thunder People. I can take you on tour. You can step inside and watch the reactions."

"Let me sleep on it first," Joslin replied, heading back toward the gate.

"Wait, Mom," Gerwyn said, tugging at her leggings. "I want to see the fusion reactions with Alfie."

Joslin leaned over and picked up her small son. "OK, but you must give me a tour tomorrow morning when I am fresh."

Gerwyn smiled, nodding his head with exuberant satisfaction. He glanced quickly at his father as his mother handed him to Alfie.

Yuri kissed his son on the forehead while Alfie held the boy. "I'm still on my honeymoon. I will be with your mother tonight. Have fun."

"Let's go," Gerwyn told Alfie after he waved his parents off.

"He's growing up quick," Joslin remarked as she watched her son disappear down a narrow corridor leading to the reactor.

"How about a cup of green tea with Freddie at the gate?" Kuan Yin asked. "There is a tea house near the Feathered Dragon."

Yuri took Joslin's arm in his, and she kissed his cheek. They accompanied Kuan Yin to the tea house. Freddie remained half asleep, which lent a relaxed ambience to the simply decorated tea house. Kuan Yin brewed several cups of tea and placed them on the small table on the floor.

Joslin took a sip and then lowered her cup briefly. "I never realized how much Dad resembled Gamaliel."

"Who was Gamaliel?" Yuri asked.

"Gamaliel taught Merilyn, the head wizard at Camelon. Merilyn was Eegan's father," Joslin explained. "Gamaliel would blow himself up with an alchemy experiment and then come back to finish it. Another one of Gamaliel's students became the only Merwyn to survive the Serpentine attack. Elissa and I rescued him. We called him Merlin."

Joslin paused for a moment before continuing. "Dad must have spent several lifetimes with this reactor after the Turkish one."

Kuan Yin looked at her and laughed. "Yes, he has been busy ever since. Unfortunately, he never left notes so the information remains sketchy."

"Ahem," Freddie interrupted as he opened the eye that had remained closed during his light slumber. "He could not leave notes otherwise the recipient would have been tracked by the Serpentine Federation. They kill those with knowledge about nuclear fusion."

Joslin sputtered her last sip of green tea. "What? Our son just went in the reactor to learn about fusion!"

Yuri began quizzing Freddie. "So why aren't we all dead now?"

"Well, you can't kill Kuan Yin in her present ascended state," Freddie quipped.

Kuan Yin shrugged and resumed sipping her tea. "Things improved. Arcas provided sketchy information this time around."

"Nothing like learning under pressure," Freddie remarked dryly.

"Many of us know about fusion," Kuan Yin added, eyeing Joslin for signs of understanding. "We just chose to forget it or keep it only on the intuitive portion of the brain. As long as you don't move the information over to the other side of the brain with a big 'Ah Ha,' you can't be tracked. Three-year-olds just know it. Gerwyn is too young for a big Ah Ha. Your dad was always on the run from the Serpentine Federation, so having the knowledge came with the territory."

"Ohhh," Joslin said, putting her cup of green tea firmly on the table. "That's the reason Dad keeps me guessing."

"Apparently no one can have all of the information at once," Yuri remarked.

"You got it," Freddie said. "He didn't want people to lose it."

"He also ran out of time," Kuan Yin acknowledged. "No one anticipated Pellinor's actions. Not even the Serpentines."

A small tear rolled down Joslin's cheek. Yuri reached for her hand to comfort her, and she lightly squeezed his palm.

"He preferred telling you about the merpeople, stars, fairies, love, and life," Kuan Yin revealed. "He wanted you to keep your life balanced. He figured that you'd find danger soon enough. You were his only hope."

Yuri smiled at her as a tear began to roll down his cheek. He rubbed Joslin's hand affectionately while she softly cried. He quietly whispered, "'Tis true. You were our only hope."

Chapter Twelve

Sometimes giving up

Everything you OWN

Is all it takes

Tune Reference: *Everything I Own*

----Bread

"WE ARE ALL fusion reactors," Gerwyn told his parents before they entered the narrow corridor leading to the fusion room. "We spiral through all the elements of life without stopping."

"What are these walls made of?" Joslin asked as they stepped inside the reactor room.

"Alfie said that they were a blend of graphite and silica," Gerwyn answered. "Nothing gets out unless it is meant to be."

"You mean that we can birth matter?" Yuri questioned.

"Oh yes," Gerwyn replied. "Alfie said so. It is how the Thunder People keep running."

"So whatever decays gets regrouped," Joslin surmised.

"That is how it works. People get sick when they get hung up on a particular element," Gerwyn explained.

"Ohhh," Joslin murmured as she studied the array of flashing lights randomly spiraling the room. "I see how lead brought down Rome."

"Alfie said that it resonated with them spiritually," Gerwyn commented.

Joslin stared at the streaks of colored lights dancing across the room. She paused briefly before continuing. "We need to put this reactor in another dimension now."

"How? And which dimension?" Yuri asked, agreeing with her assessment.

"Something based on the human form, like the carbon element," she said. "We'll need to uplift the resonance."

"Diamond dust!" Yuri exclaimed.

"Yes, it works well on my shielding cloak, and you know how often it has been road tested," she replied with chagrin.

"That is fine for the reactor in China, but what about covering the sunken crystal from Atlantis?" Yuri inquired.

"I'll use diamond dust for that too," Joslin answered.

"I wasn't talking about the diamond dust," Yuri pointed out.

"I know," Joslin said looking down at the sandy floor of the reactor room.

"There's danger involved in hiding the sunken crystal from the Serpentines," he told her.

"I know," Joslin said as she looked up from the dirt and stared Yuri in the eye. "That is why you will be accompanying Alfie and Gerwyn to the Library in Rhakotis. I will meet you there when I am done."

"You want me to escort you across the Nile portal in the virtual transition?" Yuri asked more for clarity rather than as a question.

"Yes, you can retrieve my soul," Joslin replied. "Fortunately, we are like diamonds with different facets. Otherwise, it would all be a done deal.

Watching these spiraling fusion reactions has made me realize that a part of me died with my father." She stopped momentarily and scuffed some sand on her toes. "Now I understand his loneliness."

"Your father had many facets too," Yuri remarked, scuffing more dirt on Joslin's toes. "You represented the dream that was taken from him. The worst thing that you can do to a human being is kill his or her dreams. I can't let you go."

Joslin smiled at the interaction. "It isn't just me. It isn't just Arcas. Many other beloved Camelon knights died alone and in distress."

"It is a very human thing to feel pain," Yuri commented.

"That is what we are here for," Joslin answered. "It separates us from the Serpentines."

"A facet of our dreams exist in each other," Yuri said softly. "The basis of our existence is at stake. Now I realize this. We have arrived at this point."

"It is the balance," Joslin replied. "That is most likely why the Turkish wizard put the fusion reactor in the east, where the populace specializes in questions of balance. Besides, the Sun star civilization is the nearest example of fusion around. The only problem is that the Sons of Heaven are a patriarchal society by definition. There is something to be said for finding the balance of yin and yang within oneself."

"The east is also the place where a picture speaks a thousand words," Yuri added. "There is more to know here, although the place needs your touch."

Gerwyn withdrew from the Table of the Elements that he was creating in the sand and piped in with, "Alfie said that if you know your point of arrival, then you are lost in time."

"Sorta reminds me of the first time I sang to you," Yuri purred to his wife as he moved closer to her. He pushed back her hair and softly stroked her check.

Joslin blushed slightly. "We lost track of the time that night. Everyone else had already gone to bed. You kept singing."

"I only sang one song," Yuri reminded her as he lightly kissed her cheek.

"I kno-ow-ow," Joslin quietly murmured as she slowly turned around and fused her lips with Yuri's.

"We resonated throughout the night," Yuri teased.

Gerwyn became distracted by his sand drawings and wandered across the room to complete his Table of the Elements. Out of the corner of his eye, he noticed his father lift his mother into his arms. Another thought crossed his mind as he continued his art. "Alfie said that this was a great room for passing time, especially if you wanted to wrinkle it."

His parents quit kissing, and Joslin jumped down to the ground.

"Another revelation," she told Yuri. "Good thing that I am in a relaxed mood. The little man is keeping us on track."

"I was just ready to learn more about fusion," Yuri confessed. "I'm not sure that we have finished that topic."

"Apparently we gotta catch it when we can," Joslin observed, straightening herself on the floor of the reactor room. "Study break. You were correct earlier. There is more to know here."

"What do you know about time wrinkles?" Gerwyn's father asked him.

"I dunno," Gerwyn replied nonchalantly as he surveyed the progression of his artwork. "I want to copy my art on the papyrus. In order to fit it all in, I must fold the papyrus paper. The fold will wrinkle it."

Joslin sat down in the sand next to Gerwyn and sighed. "Dad mentioned a time wrinkle. He told me that he had made one before he ever pulled the sword from the stone. He did it when his grandfather, King Cole, died."

Yuri sat down next to Joslin on the ground. Taking a deep breath, he admitted, "Ivan told me that King Cole died under mysterious circumstances."

"Serpentines ambushed him," Joslin explained. "They don't like merry ol' souls."

"Why?" Yuri demanded.

"It threatens their existence. He couldn't be hooked," Joslin explained. "They exist on codependency."

"This means that the time wrinkles separate us from the Serpentines," Yuri surmised.

"We are known by our choices rather than by who we are," Joslin said. "Choice affects the outcome."

"Now I understand our further vulnerability," Yuri reasoned.

"Dad also said that dinosaurs scream loudest before they fall," Joslin added.

"I see that the heat is on," Yuri answered. "May I suggest dropping class over a romantic dinner? Alfie can come and assist Gerwyn with his papyrus copy."

Joslin caught Gerwyn's eye and winked at him. Gerwyn smiled when he saw her but remained focused on his art. He told them, "I'm busy."

Chapter Thirteen

Sometimes all it takes

Is a change in perspective

From a forbidden place

Tune Reference: *Up On A Roof*

----James Taylor

JOSLIN LINGERED IN bed for a few moments the next morning. Yuri had risen early and went to brew some tea in the adjacent tea house room. Gerwyn and Alfie had fallen asleep on the mats in the other room.

He returned with a tray of refreshments and sat down on the futon near Joslin. "Now that you've had a night to sleep on it, have you changed the details of your plans?"

"No, you don't get off that easy. You are still hanging out at the library with Alfie and Gerwyn," she said, sipping her tea. Then she raised her head. "I know what I am doing."

"I know," he acknowledged softly. "Let's get away from the reactor for a moment. How about having breakfast on the roof overlooking the palace courtyard? We can sit next to Ivan and Elissa."

"Better yet, we'll send the dragons to the palace kitchen for breakfast," Joslin suggested with a slightly playful arch of her back.

The happy couple summoned their Sea Dragons for a ride to the top of the high tiled roof. Only Ivan answered their call. He appeared extremely happy, though disheveled. His fur stood erect in random areas of his body, and there was dust on his diamond-studded claws.

"Hey, my man, you look like you've been up all night!" Yuri exclaimed, patting Ivan on the back as he lifted Joslin onto the tiger-like dragon.

"Elissa laid eggs," he announced with a proud twinkle in his eye. "She is nesting with them on the roof."

"Eggs!" Joslin cried as she rose and danced on top of Ivan. She held her hand out to help Yuri climb onto Ivan's back. "We have new Sea Dragon eggs. No wonder we felt attracted to the roof. Let's go! Up on the roof!"

Yuri pulled Joslin back down on the Sea Dragon as he settled on Ivan's back. "Gerwyn will be so happy. He has been on a mission to find Dragon eggs ever since we began the honeymoon. It is about time he bonded with nestlings."

"We have an entire new generation of Dragon flyers to raise," Joslin announced while they soared in the air over the palace. "Arthur's son, Dewi, is ready to raise nestlings too. He is in the monastery that Patrick runs in Wales. We'll have to change the operations in Wales and Ireland after we put the sunken Atlantean crystal in another dimension."

"How do you figure?" Yuri asked in a perplexed voice.

"Tell you later," she whispered as Ivan landed on the roof. "We need to settle the nestlings first."

The couple dismounted and joined Elissa near the seven dragon eggs. Elissa looked up at them with extreme joy on her face, after having produced the first nest of Sea Dragon eggs since pre-Atlantean times. Only the Furry and Feathered Dragons had provided the world with dragons after Atlantis collapsed.

Joslin and Yuri embraced Elissa and congratulated her and Ivan on their new family. Joslin kneeled over the nest made out of hay borrowed from the horses' stalls. She and Yuri examined the eggs for signs of health.

"Oh, they are so beautiful," Joslin told Elissa. "They glitter like the stars in the sky. I can't wait to meet the new arrivals."

"Ivan and I were so inspired by you and Yuri," Elissa replied. "We wanted children of our own."

"We'll have to make it look like he made a major discovery," Ivan said with a slightly mischievous smile.

"He'll like that," Joslin answered, rising from the nest to stand next to Elissa. "He hasn't put it all together yet, though he knows he is on a mission. It is time for a new generation of Dragon flyers."

"I know," Elissa softly said as she looked down at the silent eggs. "I sensed that the sunken Atlantean crystal and fusion reactor must be placed in another dimension. That is your next mission."

Joslin hung her head a little. She never could hide anything from Elissa. The Golden Sea Dragon queen never quit overseeing planetary affairs. Now she understood why Elissa had chosen a roof for a nest. The next generation must be raised with a bird's-eye perspective.

Raising her head to look the Golden Sea Dragon queen directly in the eye, she acknowledged, "Yes, I was just telling Yuri of the plan."

"Great," Elissa quietly said. "I'm glad that you are on it. When do we leave for the Yucatan Peninsula?"

"Do you mean to say that the new dragon eggs get covered in diamond dust too?"

"Yes, my dear," Elissa confirmed with a slight air of resignation. "I knew that they were earmarked for another dimension when I laid them. I just had that feeling about them, especially with the recent Serpentine threat."

"We'll hatch them in the other dimension and bring them out for Gerwyn and his classmates in the monasteries," Ivan interjected.

Joslin listened thoughtfully, weighing the change in plans. Then she consented. "All right, we'll be flexible. Ivan, you can accompany Gerwyn and Yuri to the Rhakotis Library. Elissa and I will put everything in another dimension under the Serpentines' noses with a little diamond dust. Gerwyn's dragon egg hunt will just have to wait for the time being."

"I think he can handle it," Yuri speculated.

"Excuse us," Joslin apologized to the Sea Dragons. "It is a parenting moment." Then she turned toward Yuri. "You may be right. We'll tell him that the eggs must go someplace else to hatch. It will give him some sense of bonding and something else to anticipate."

"He'll like the thought of going to school to learn dragon care. It is about time he meets his cousins," Yuri added.

"OK, we're done," Joslin decided. "So much for a romantic breakfast for two, but this is another exciting distraction."

Yuri tossed his hands in the air with a little sigh. "We'll catch up later." Facing Ivan with a wry smile, he instructed, "Go get Alfie and Gerwyn to help you bring breakfast to the roof. It is time to celebrate. Tell Gerwyn that you are taking him to a surprise birthday party for his new friends. We'll take it from there."

Ivan flew off the roof in a hurry. He returned a half hour later with Gerwyn and Alfie. Gerwyn raced to the dragon eggs as Alfie produced two sacks of prepared food and began distributing the contents.

"Oh look! Dragon eggs!" Gerwyn shouted, clapping his small hands in delight. He posed himself in front of the nest so that he could touch the eggs with his little fingers. "Mom, Dad, they are warm! It must be their birthday. Happy birthday…happy birthday!"

Joslin smiled as she watched her son. "OK, Gerwyn. It is your job to help pack them up for their new nest on the Yucatan Peninsula. When they hatch and get a little bigger, you can go to school with them."

"Ohhh!" Gerwyn cooed excitedly. "All my very own." He began sorting the eggs and found one to lift inside Elissa's pouch. Ivan ran to assist the small boy, and together they carefully placed the Dragon eggs against Elissa's warm scales.

Joslin kissed Yuri good-bye and swiftly climbed aboard Elissa's back. Alfie handed her a jar of diamond dust from the kitchen. Waving at Gerwyn, she braced herself and flew over the fusion reactor. The diamond dust fell on the building like shiny silver raindrops. Everything the dust touched vanished before their eyes, including Freddie.

"Don't worry," Yuri assured his son. He lifted the boy onto Ivan's back. "It will return to our eyesight when the time is right. Like the wind, you will always be able to feel its presence, though you can't see it."

Alfie joined Yuri on Ivan's soft, furry back. Flying high into the setting sun, they waved farewell to the emperor, who was watching from a nearby porch, and the rapidly disappearing Feathered Dragon. Fire and puffs of smoked billowed from the invisible Feathered Dragon below them. Soon a cloud shielded them from the city below.

Meanwhile, Joslin and Elissa headed for the Yucatan Peninsula.

Chapter Fourteen

The lively art of

Having history repeat itself

To determine

What is really essential

Tune Reference: *Return To Pooh Corner*

----Kenny Loggins

WHEN JOSLIN REACHED the landing pad at the Yucatan Peninsula, she carefully unloaded the dragon eggs and nested them in the barracks. It was nighttime, and darkness covered the region. She found a straw bed in the barracks and fell asleep near the eggs. Early the next morning, she rose and searched for a Feathered Dragon in another barrack.

"I'll take the white one over there," she told the Mayan caretaker. "It won't be long. I'm still on my honeymoon and gotta get back to my babes."

Without further words, she settled on the back of the White-Feathered Dragon, and they flew above the site. She sprinkled diamond dust over the entire facility and then headed for the sunken Atlantean crystal in the Caribbean basin. Her diamond-threaded armor reflected her surroundings. The Serpentines on the nearby islands below would not be able to see her, though they could possibly detect her presence with their radar systems. She knew they had not evolved fast enough to match the changing consciousness of the past generation. The White-Feathered Dragon nodded at her when they soared over the crystal. Using the gift of vision that the Sea Dragons had bestowed upon her during a training exercise, she easily outlined the shadow of the crystal marring the water's clear surface.

She noticed a slight buzzing in her ears and wriggled uncomfortably on the back of the Feathered Dragon. The electromagnetic frequencies that were being emitted distorted the polarized magnetite in her occiput, causing her to feel disoriented. The white, birdlike dragon shook her head slightly to reset her own internal compass. Like other birds and humans, the Feathered Dragons possessed magnetite in their skulls, which provided a sense of true north.

Joslin sprinkled diamond dust over the outline of the sunken crystal as the Feathered Dragon made several swoops over the area. To an outside observer, the dragon's graceful motions resembled those of a gull diving for fish. Only a trained eye would notice that the gull was really a large dragon.

When the task was complete, they hurried back to the Yucatan Peninsula, where the facility remained hidden from view. The Feathered Dragon, remembering the exact longitude and latitude, landed near a grove of blooming plumerias. Joslin recognized the site by its smell. The grinning Mayan caretaker came into view and escorted the White-Feathered Dragon back to the barracks. Joslin watched them disappear into thin air in the middle of the grove. Satisfied that she had accomplished her mission, she ducked behind two plumeria trees and headed down the portal to the library at Rhakotis.

When Joslin arrived, she found Yuri singing Gerwyn a lullaby. The drowsy young boy greeted his mother with a warm hug and kiss. Then, closing his eyes, his head sank back down on the pillow. He sighed deeply before smiling contentedly. "'Night, Mommy."

Yuri kissed her on the head as she leaned over her son. "Good to see you."

Joslin rose as Gerwyn fell asleep. Yuri saw him nod off, and he led Joslin out of the alcove.

Outside the room, they quietly embraced with a long, tender kiss.

Yuri whispered, "I have some things to show you. We've made a few discoveries. Follow me. Let's stop by the kitchen and get something to eat first. You'll need some refreshment before the next step in this odyssey."

Joslin grabbed a bowl of soup and silently ate it in the kitchen. She tried to relax, but the momentum of events kept her alert. Yuri sat across from her at the table while he thumbed through a leather-bound book of papyrus. He showed Joslin a curious diagram on a page slightly beyond the middle of the book.

She recognized the image, and her eyes widened. "It's a map of all the tunnels in the Arctos cave system, which covers a third of Asia. It is far more extensive than I thought."

"Me too," Yuri replied as he turned the book toward him for further examination while she ate.

Joslin began to relax with the realization that help was only just across the table. The meal began to slow her thinking process, which was for the better. She took a deep breath and released the tension in her shoulders. After a few sips of her tea, she rose and announced, "Let's go. I'm ready."

Following Yuri down a long corridor, she began to notice the pictures lining the walls. Unable to make out their designs, she hurried to catch up with Yuri's quickening steps. He opened a heavy graphite door to a room of granite rubble.

"It's radioactive," he cautioned her. "It is from Connemara, Ireland."

Joslin stepped back.

"It's all right as long as you don't stay long," he told her. "I dreamed about this room while we were resting near the fusion reactor in China."

Joslin cocked her head to one side. "Do I hear water?"

"Yes, a tiny underground stream comes through here. I have been searching through the library for information on its purpose and course," he revealed. "Our exposure time is up. Let's get out of here."

"No, there's information in these rocks," Joslin said, stepping back to study the contents of the room.

"I know. The communication will stay in your memory and come through in your dreams," he explained. "There's a marble room next door. It also is radioactive. Apparently it morphed from the radioactive limestone in the room next to it. The marble is from the Inagh Valley in Connemara."

"OK, now I am ready to leave," Joslin admitted. "It is due more to information overload than radiation overexposure. I think that I'll sleep on the rest."

The next morning, Joslin met with Yuri at breakfast. Gerwyn had already eaten and played nearby with Ivan. Joslin sat down beside Yuri and slowly sipped a cup of green tea. Her dreams had been lucid, and she felt a little groggy.

"What did you dream?" Yuri asked, looking up from the book that he was perusing.

"I dreamed that the stream in the granite room led to a sacred healing temple in ancient Egypt," Joslin slowly began. "The runoff never saw the light of day and filled a basin in an underground room. Humans used the waters to correct distortions in the human form wrought by Serpentine interference."

"Hmm." Yuri reflected. "The drawings on the corridor wall illustrate your dream."

"You're right," Joslin answered. "I'll check them out after breakfast."

Alfie entered the kitchen from the corridor and sat down next to Joslin. "I heard you mention the artwork in the corridor. There's a story behind it."

"Well, let's have it," Joslin demanded. "I think that is our next clue."

"There is a portal behind the limestone room," Alfie said. "It leads to the library underneath Marlboro's town square."

Joslin groaned. Her father, King Arcas, had barely escaped crucifixion in the Marlboro town square. She had no desire to revisit the scene.

Yuri noticed her discomfort. "We can stay underground in the library," he suggested. "No need to haunt Marlboro at this moment in history. Marlboro has had a rough go of it lately."

Joslin wryly grinned in retrospect and changed her perspective. "My father led the uprising there. No need to bother them tonight. There is a monastery there that we can visit. Meanwhile, Alfie can return to Britain after he helps us piece together the story of the healing radioactive waters. I hear that my brother, King Arthur, needs a hand in the north while he handles the south. The Serpentines have become more troublesome in the regions. Gerwyn can help Elissa nest the dragon eggs from the Yucatan portal."

"You mean my babysitting days are over?" Alfie smiled.

"For the moment," Joslin acknowledged. "We can take it from here. Gerwyn has found his dragon eggs, and that will keep him focused. England needs you, but let's go study some art first."

They left the kitchen together and entered the corridor to the rock rooms.

"Our story begins with the intergalactic wars of ancient Egypt," Alfie narrated after he had examined the first drawing. "The Serpentine experiments began to grossly modify the human forms. Some of the pharaohs suffered major genetic anomalies as a result. Their human features became distorted, passing down to their progeny."

"The rebellion during the time of Moses went underground," Joslin continued. "They found that the waters contaminated with debris from a missile attack counteracted the Serpentine results. The missiles were from the Sirius star system, the Black Dog occult group that had infiltrated ancient Egypt. They operated the temples above ground. The Black Dog occult group had first attacked the Conn Druid tribe in present-day Ireland. They were tracking down Lemurian refugees and killed any humans that aided them. The area resisted, and the Black Dog occult group retreated to the pyramid bases in Egypt."

"In the hands of a skilled physician, these waters offset genetic damage from radioactive contamination," Joslin observed. "Enough for now. Let's get going in Britain. Everyone grab a flask of the healing waters. We may need it later."

Alfie departed for northern Britain when they reached the exit for Marlboro. Joslin and Yuri remained underground and roamed the library stacks. In one of the reading rooms, they found a slumped figure at a study table.

Joslin examined the body for signs of life and recognized the face. "It is the mother superior from the local nunnery. She's barely breathing."

Joslin moistened the woman's lips with a drop from the healing radioactive waters. The woman slowly rolled her head around, and her eyes opened slightly. Then she closed them again and dropped her head on the table.

Joslin stepped away as the woman stirred again. While keeping her head still, she managed to stretch her upper body. Then she moaned, "I lost Pellinor."

"Ohh," Joslin responded, stepping away from the nun. "Somebody saved your life by placing you in this dimension. You look like you've been nuked."

"I feel like I've been nuked," the woman answered as she raised her head and glanced at Yuri and Joslin. "I gotta get back to the nunnery. I kept an eye on Pellinor as part of the exchange."

"What exchange?" Yuri asked.

"Being a descendant of Joseph of Arimathea, they went light on him," the nun explained. "After defeating the traitorous King Lot and his army, he lost his mind and betrayed the Knights of Camelon in a time wrinkle. He trapped them in the intergalactic wars of ancient Egypt. The surviving knights asked me to get as much technical information from him as possible."

"So where is Pellinor now?" Yuri questioned before turning to Joslin. "Is this guy an in-law or distant relation?"

"Outlaw now." Joslin shrugged. "And distant in many ways."

"He introduced some Serpentines to the nunnery, and they took over," the nun explained. "Somehow they bridged the building to the radioactive stores of the local Black Dog occult group, and the entire convent became a fission reactor, which isn't as safe as a fusion one. The energy reached the apatite concentrates left millions of years ago in the bedrock under the monastery. The time wrinkle that they were trying to produce rebounded. They got time warped instead, and I got nuked on the emotional plane. I have protection as long as I keep my spirits up. It broke my heart to see what Pellinor did to the place. I love books, so I came down here to recover. Meanwhile, a Reptilian spaceship took Pellinor away."

"Did you get its license number?" Joslin asked eagerly.

"Yes, I wrote it down in that papyrus pad over there," the nun said. "Only those with great density went with the spaceship. The lighter ones entered another dimension and escaped to the library. The others are snoozing in the study rooms down the aisle."

"I can understand why Dad wanted us to come here," Joslin remarked to Yuri as they scurried down the aisle. "This is an emergency, whether Mother Superior realizes it or not. It must have happened around the time of Eegan's murder."

"After we wake the others, let's get back to Gerwyn and the nestlings," Yuri suggested.

"I agree," Joslin murmured. "There's no place like home."

Chapter Fifteen

A life without meaning
Is a life unlived

Tune Reference: *(I've Been) Searchin' So Long*
----Chicago

"WELL, IT APPEARS that there has been a major shift with the nunneries," Joslin commented when they were back at the Rhakotis Library. "The rest of the orders will hear about this event."

Yuri nodded as they sipped some herb tea while watching Gerwyn care for the dragon eggs. The small boy enjoyed rearranging them in the nest and keeping them warm next to Elissa.

"It is time to pay Patrick another visit at the monastery in Wales," Elissa advised. Obviously, the hormones of motherhood had not clouded her analytical abilities.

"That's a great idea," Joslin replied.

"Look, one of the dragon eggs is beginning to crack!" Gerwyn exclaimed.

"I think one of the little pipers overheard our plans," Ivan remarked. Taking a deep breath, he roared at the others in a deep, patriarchal voice. "C'mon, kiddos, get a move on it. Your mother is needed in Wales."

"Oh, Ivan!" Elissa sighed dreamily as the rest of the dragon eggs started cracking. "They know the sound of their papa."

Joslin rolled her eyes, purposely ignoring the rapport between the two Sea Dragons. She pushed Gerwyn closer to the hatching dragon eggs just as the first Sea Dragon emerged from his shell.

"Look, I can see right through the baby dragon!" Gerwyn shouted excitedly.

"That's my boy!" Ivan roared with pride. "He's transparent."

Joslin stepped away from the nest to get a different perspective. Yuri slowly sipped his herb tea and thoughtfully gazed at the sight without a word. All seven dragons arrived transparent.

"Congratulations," Yuri softly said to the parents. "You two managed to go where no other dragon has gone before."

Elissa beamed while Ivan warmly rubbed her shoulders. He silently nodded his satisfaction. Each transparent dragon had a unique hue, like the protoplasm of a jellyfish.

"The first one's name is Smoke! He is mine," Gerwyn insisted, delightedly clasping his little hands together over his heart.

Smoke tottered over to Gerwyn and gave him a little puff. The puff exposed the baby Sea Dragon with his gray fur coat, which shimmered in the smoky light like diamonds.

"Look, I can see him when he smokes!" Gerwyn shouted in amazement.

"We'll bring the one with the blue protoplasm," Joslin decided. "We'll take just one at a time."

****

Six weeks later, Joslin packed the blue transparent dragon in Elissa's pouch, and they headed for Wales. Patrick, the bishop, greeted Queen Joslin at the door and quickly ushered her into the small one-room cottage. He peered over her shoulder for a glimpse of the nestling. Elissa remained hidden behind a stall while she pushed Blue, the transparent dragon, forward with a quickly evaporating cloud of smoke.

"Oh my!" he excitedly said. "What a change!" Then he winked at Joslin. "We knew that we were due for a dramatic one."

"What is it with the transparency bit?" she questioned Patrick as she sat down in a chair near the hearth.

"Why, you, of course," Patrick replied, stoking the fire. Then, without further explanation, he changed the subject. "I hear that you have been on an odyssey concerning your father. I have a clue for you."

"Yes, it is like a scavenger hunt, but the stakes are big," she replied, staring into the fire.

"I know," Patrick answered. "That's why he set it up the way he did. At least, someone did set it up."

The wizened man retrieved something from a box on the mantel. He produced a huge clear diamond the size of Alfie's fist. The large stone reflected the light of the fire. Handing the stone to Joslin, he told her, "Soul love is transparent. This stone conducts signals of a higher vibrational frequency than what can be heard by the Serpentines or Grays. The communication is invisible because they are too dense to hear it."

"All the new dragons can hear those frequencies," Joslin surmised.

"Precisely," Patrick said. "We speculated that we would get there sooner or later. This is how we can escape detection from the latest Serpentine activities and Eye-in-the-Sky."

"As long as we communicate without coloring the message of love, then we can't be found," Joslin observed.

"You and your family, both living and dead, have birthed transparency into the world at a critical time," Patrick continued. "We will all hide behind it."

Joslin stayed the night, going over Patrick's words in her dreams as she slept by the hearth. Meanwhile, he arranged for Dewi, King Arthur's son by Non, to meet Blue. The six-year-old boy found the transparent dragon in the horse stall when he went to clean it the next morning. Joslin emerged from behind one of the horses.

"How's my nephew?" she greeted. "It is time for you to learn dragon care."

Dewi embraced his aunt and stared in awe at the transparent nestling. Only a hint of blue filled the shape of the dragon. Most untrained people would disregard the blue hue in the air as a mist, cloud, or smoke from a nearby fire or chimney.

"Here," Elissa said as she appeared from a stall in a puff of smoke that illuminated Blue's true form.

"Wow! She's beautiful!" Dewi cried.

After teaching Dewi the basics of Dragon care, Joslin left with Elissa.

"We'll bring the others one by one," she promised Dewi. "Gerwyn will join you when he turns five."

Then she and Elissa flew away underneath cloud cover. They returned to the Rhakotis Library, where Joslin handed Elissa over to her caretaker for grooming. Joslin remained with Elissa to continue brainstorming with her.

"I wanted to spruce up before seeing Ivan and the children," Elissa explained. She turned her head toward Joslin and asked, "What are you going to do with the diamond communicator?"

"Go visit the nunnery at Marlboro," Joslin replied. "They could use a soul retrieval as well as a new convent. The townsfolk think that the nuns ascended to heaven with angels. They don't know about Pellinor and his space lift. For all they know, he died in the town fire years ago. Mother Superior elicited information from him as part of the exchange for accessing the Marlboro Library."

"We can use the stone to help block Pellinor's escape route so that the Serpentines don't track the nuns and return through the same energetic opening that he left," Elissa suggested.

"Great idea. We'll hide all of our schools in other convents and monasteries," Joslin agreed.

"How about placing Mother Superior and her nuns at a local convent near Dewi?" Elissa asked. "He could use a mother's touch."

"There's another great idea, especially since Mother Superior will be suffering from empty-nest syndrome. She babied Pellinor, and he took advantage of the situation. Elissa, you should lay eggs more often," Joslin happily replied. She began rubbing her hands together and lightly danced on her feet like her young son. "Mother Superior knows the lore and can impart the information she gleaned from Pellinor. Our young Dragon flyers will get an incredible education."

"The best for our young." Elissa beamed.

"Let's get going after I check on Gerwyn," Joslin decided. "We'll bring Yuri and Ivan. A masculine voice will catch their attention, and I'll put Yuri in charge. We've got some nuns to move."

Elissa eyed her and cocked her head to the side.

"On second thought, you and I can meet the nuns at the monastery in Wales," Joslin said as she noticed Elissa's questioning glance. "We wouldn't want to be a distraction, would we?"

Elissa nodded her satisfaction with the strategy. "I think they will really enjoy their new location next to the monastery in Wales. Only the Serpentines assume that the inhabitants resort to celibacy."

"Otherwise, they would change the entire genetic content with theirs," Joslin said. "Patrick is walking a fine line. The Serpentine authorities killed all of his progeny with his wife. He is on a mission. He knows that they will devour whatever they cannot claim as theirs."

"So we must now hide our young," Elissa observed.

"Yes," Joslin nodded. "Arthur's life partner, Non, returned to the area to be closer to her son. Whenever Arthur visits, he disguises himself as a monk. Mother Superior will be relocated to Non's convent. Non leaves whenever Ceredig returns to the region. Mother Superior can help the convent with those who seek refuge."

"They are raising the future rulers of Wales, Ireland, Scotland, England, Germany, France, and the Norse country," Elissa remarked.

"And their knights and Dragon flyers," Joslin added.

"It is a secular tradition," Elissa observed.

"We save our souls from the Serpentines as well as our genes," Joslin acknowledged. "It isn't simple."

"I see the reason for the transparency," Elissa admitted.

"It's our only hope," Joslin reminded her.

"Let's bring a second transparent dragon to the monastery. Save a trip," Elissa offered.

"That's another great idea." Joslin smiled. "How about Pinkie? He complements Blue if you look at gender integration. Besides, Arthur's Sea Dragon, Alfred, is hot pink. The color scheme will work for the moment until the other refugees arrive."

Chapter Sixteen

Celebrate the simple things in life

Tune Reference: *Mother And Child Reunion*

----Paul Simon

JOSLIN AND ELISSA met Mother Superior at the horse stall near Patrick's cottage. Yuri and eight men from his Dragon flyer group accompanied them. They had brought over twenty nuns from the nunnery near Marlboro. Leaving the male escorts behind, the women clustered around the ten children standing with Dewi and the transparent dragons.

"I think they are feeling more maternal than romantic," Yuri observed as watched the interactions of the assorted groups.

Joslin nodded her agreement. "Well, it is what we need right now. We must take care of our young."

"This is a much better arrangement for us," Mother Superior reflected. "After the Castle Marlboro fell, we came under scrutiny."

"It is time to heal the Maimed King," Joslin announced, changing the subject.

"My father, King Pelles?" Mother Superior questioned. "Lancelot fell in love with his niece. His son, Galahad, often went fishing with him."

"Same principle," Joslin said.

"You're right," Mother Superior admitted. "Galahad was like a grandson. There's nothing more healing to a wounded old man than the demands of a vital young boy. He helped Dad literally get back on his feet again."

"The Roman soldiers took out King Pelles at the knees," Joslin explained to Yuri. "However, he remained active and got around in a boat. They nicknamed him the Fisher King because he would bring things to him with a fishing pole. Everything fell under the spell of his hook, especially Roman soldiers."

"So he wasn't so incapacitated after all," Yuri commented.

"He became the Romans' worst enemy," Joslin continued.

Mother Superior nodded. "He took back his kingdom by hook and by crook."

"Romans don't do so well when they are in the water," Joslin elaborated. "Nobody ever teaches them how to swim. King Pelles would go fishing with Romans and never bothered to reel them in. He took out a couple of fleets with the mermaids providing a distraction. The Romans blamed it on a Loch Ness monster, but it really was King Pelles with a vengeance. Little Nellie, the Sea Dragon, just stepped into the vacancy that King Pelles left after his fishing days ceased. The Romans were too proud to admit that someone who couldn't even march to a drumbeat had beaten them. You know how fond they are of roads and bridges. It was the Serpentine influence. They could only think in lines."

"Hmm, they never considered the possibility that someone could forge his or her own trail, much less waterways," Yuri observed.

"The locals are too creative for trails," Mother Superior reflected. "Some walk, some fly, some swim, some ride, some wander…"

A group of woodsmen entered the stalls and interrupted her train of thought. One of them turned and winked at Mother Superior as he quickly threw a black robe over his head. Sensing that no further introductions would be needed, Yuri and Joslin backed away.

"Elissa, time to go." Joslin hastened away.

Yuri waved his group of Dragon flyers off. "I think they can take it from here, men. Thanks for your help with the nuns. Catch ya' in Utopia after the honeymoon!"

Yuri's friends grinned and flew under cloud cover to their base in the Altai Mountains. Joslin hugged and kissed her nephew good-bye. She nodded at Mother Superior, who had started planning a cookout for the evening. Joslin managed to catch her eye.

"Are you sure that you don't want to stay for dinner?" Mother Superior asked her with a smile.

"No, thank you," Joslin replied. "We are going to follow up on the Fisher King angle before heading back."

"OK, sounds good. See ya' soon," Mother Superior answered as she bustled about with dinner preparations."

Joslin climbed on Elissa's back while Yuri boarded Ivan. Together they flew toward northern England in the dusk. By the time they landed in present-day Cornwall, they were cloaked in darkness. A familiar figure emerged from the forest and lowered the hood on his cape.

"How's it going, Alfie?" Joslin whispered as she embraced her former babysitter.

"I think we have a secure kingdom here," Alfie replied. "The Romans think that the Britons and Saxons are fighting each other. We just finished having a wonderful bonfire with your cousins, the Saxons. The remaining

Roman soldiers fled the scene, yelling something about barbarians and chaos."

"They are so linear." Joslin sighed. "They never could handle our parties."

"They don't know how to have a good time. All they do is overeat and vomit." Alfie reflected for a moment. "It works to our advantage."

"Oh well, maybe someday we'll get around to writing our own history," Joslin added. "We are too busy making history. Everyone knows that the Britons get along with the Saxons. The Serpentine Romans are just trying to hide the fact that they don't get along with anyone."

"How about staying the night?" Alfie offered. "I have an extra hut. People have quieted for the night. The Romans think that the Saxons are all dead, but really we are in bed with the Saxons. It was a great party."

"Thank you so much," Joslin replied. "It was a long day moving the Marlboro convent, but they will be much happier in their new location in Wales."

"Here, come sit by my fire," Alfie suggested as he ushered them into his sod house.

Yuri accompanied Joslin inside. Elissa and Ivan remained outside, foraging in the woods. They were very skilled at scaring away curious Romans. Yuri surveyed the encampment with his cat-like eyes. The Sea Dragons would lend extra protection for the evening.

However, late in the night, after they had gone to bed, Yuri suddenly awoke with an eerie feeling. He sat up straight as an arrow in bed. Joslin remained sleeping beside him, undisturbed. Then he heard a low rumbling growl echo through the campsite.

"It's the Blues from Vega," he whispered as he shook Joslin gently awake. "We've got to get out of here before King Mark returns to Cornwall. They like to make us think they are the center of the universe, which is why the Grays sent them to inhabit Vega. Not all roads lead to the center of their universe, much less Rome. Let's go before they change our magnetics around from true north."

Joslin silently gathered their things as Yuri went to wake Alfie, who slept on the other side of the curtain in the living area. Within seconds, Alfie donned his armor and weapons before rushing out. Joslin poured water over the hearth to extinguish the embers left in the fire. She met Yuri in the woods. Despite the darkness, she knew that the entire encampment had been alerted. Though she could not see it with her dragon-like vision, she could sense the swift movement that soothed her concern.

She mounted Elissa and whispered to Yuri, "It's nice to sleep with someone who has ears like a cat. Let's get back to Gerwyn."

"My sentiments exactly," he agreed while climbing on Ivan's furry back. "Let's keep moving. This means that there will be one less attack elsewhere."

"Yes, time to reel in," Joslin insisted. "Alfie has the advantage of expecting a surprise attack."

Chapter Seventeen

Teenage wastelands

Are problems

Tune Reference: *Baba O'Reilly*

----The Who

YURI AND JOSLIN entered the Rhakotis Library and met Gerwyn in the section designated for the nestlings. He busily attended to Smoke while a caretaker dropped water over the baby dragon's body to help Gerwyn visualize him. His parents paused briefly at the door to watch the sight.

"Smoke is training you to visualize the unseen," the caretaker explained as the transparent dragon disappeared into an ephemeral haze. He shook the water off like a wet puppy.

"Now you seem him. Now you don't," Yuri said, scooping his small son into his arms for a hug.

Joslin kissed Gerwyn on the forehead while his father held him. "Looks like you've been working hard. The place is all wet. Reminds me of when I bathed you as a baby. Water, water everywhere, except for on Yuri."

Gerwyn laughed and looked up at his father. Smoke puffed a little and appeared at Gerwyn's side. With another puff, he offered a greeting for Joslin and Yuri.

"Mommy, Daddy, did you know that Smoke glows in the rock room?" Gerwyn asked. "I was looking at the pictures on the walls and noticed that they had some dragons that reminded me of Smoke."

"What?" Joslin asked, perplexed. "Will you show me?"

Yuri carefully lowered Gerwyn to the floor. The small boy ran out of the room and hurried down the corridor. His parents and Smoke followed close behind.

"See it here?" Gerwyn proudly pointed out the likeness.

"We need to ask Smoke's parents about this," Joslin decided. "I considered Smoke as an evolutionary original, but he really has his ancestors' gift for transparency."

Gerwyn continued down the corridor and opened the door to the Granite room. "C'mon, Smoke. Show 'em your stuff."

Curious, Joslin entered the granite room with Gerwyn and saw a shimmering silver dragon in the middle of the room. "Why, Smoke, you have your mother's sparkling eyes and your father's silky coat."

Smoke proudly beamed. "You can see that Elissa and Ivan played their parts very well."

"Look, Joslin!" Yuri cried. "It is another clue from your father. His name is at the bottom of this long, cryptic note."

Joslin continued to stare at Smoke. She wanted to fix the image of the shimmering dragon in her mind before he disappeared out the corridor. She called to Yuri with a puzzled expression on her face. "Are you sure that you are not hallucinating?"

"I am getting to know your father better than you," he retorted. "It is like having an ongoing man-to-man conversation, except the other man isn't here. Only the art, humor, and his sense of timing remain."

"I'm sorry, Yuri," Joslin apologized. She removed Gerwyn and Smoke from the radioactive room before joining Yuri beside the wall pictures.

The small boy and his dragon haze scurried down the corridor for further adventures. Soon he was out of sight, leaving his parents to decipher the wall pictures together on their honeymoon. Yuri pointed out the lettering to Joslin.

"You are getting cranky," he told his wife.

"The radiation gets to me quickly," she explained. "I lose patience with children, vaporizing dragons, and lost fathers."

"The note is intended for his children, not thieves like Pellinor, who break into caches of information uninvited," he reminded her. "He had to be careful. Look at what happened to Mother Superior. This stuff is loaded in an intergalactic sort of way where spaceships fly with explosive big bangs."

"What a poet you are!" she told him. "Never mind the mind-boggling technology."

"You need to take a break," he replied in response to her sarcasm.

"You are right," Joslin said as she slowly left and walked down the corridor.

Her steps were altered by the sight of a blue nun who appeared at the end of the corridor. The blue nun frantically waved at Joslin and Yuri. Joslin recognized the woman as one of the nuns from Mother Superior's convent.

"Pellinor is dead," the blue nun shouted. "The Serpentines killed him and left him in front of the Marlboro Castle."

"Well, there is no honor amongst thieves," Joslin reminded the blue nun.

"It scared the local inhabitants of Marlboro," the blue nun explained. "Many more are switching their allegiance to the Serpentine Roman government."

"Do you mean the Holy Roman Empire?" Joslin questioned. "The Holy Roman Empire is neither holy nor Roman, remember?"

"You are right," the blue nun answered. "Please forgive me. I know what Pellinor and his associates did to your father."

"No forgiveness necessary," Joslin reminded her and smiled. "The news about Pellinor is the best that I've heard all day. The body is a booby trap, though. I suspect that it is a portal to realms that we do not have the strength to defeat."

"Meanwhile, his lands go to waste," the blue nun mourned. "There is an exodus of young people from southern England heading farther south."

"Initially, the Grail knights chose to look within to find their treasure," Joslin commented. "They have been infiltrated by Pellinor's teenage sons, though we are making headway. Tell Mother Superior that Alfie is restoring Scandinavia and northern England in the manner of the Fisher King. She will understand."

Elissa suddenly appeared next to the blue nun at the far end of the corridor. "Is someone questioning Smoke's lineage?" she politely asked.

"We saw this picture and wondered whether Smoke was a virgin birth," Joslin answered, rubbing her eyes as if she had seen enough for one day.

"I assure you, most certainly not," Elissa stated. "Are we all having fun now?"

"No," Yuri said, glancing at Joslin.

Joslin met Yuri's and Elissa's gazes. She evaded their stares and instructed the blue nun. "Let me finish things here first. Please go help yourself to some refreshments in the kitchen. The caretakers can assist you in finding a place to rest. I'll get back to you in a day or two."

The blue nun grinned slightly and turned toward the kitchen. Within seconds, she was gone from view and Elissa sauntered down the hall. The golden Sea Dragon queen dropped her stare and examined the cryptic note that Yuri had been studying.

"Now, my dear," Elissa began to Joslin, "you remember the handwriting that your father taught you?"

"Yes, I know," Joslin sighed. "I'll go get my mirror from my things. Hold on."

"She's being difficult, you know," Yuri mentioned.

"She just needs to get back to her honeymoon," Elissa insisted. "The strain has been a bit too much, I suspect. She knows what this means but doesn't want to read it in black and white."

"It figures," Yuri remarked.

"Just start singing and playing your oud when we are done. She'll come around," Elissa instructed.

Yuri nodded. "I'll leave you two alone then. I have better things to do."

He quickly rose and left the corridor with a much lighter step than when he had entered. Close to the entrance, he began humming a soft, romantic tune. Then he disappeared, going in the opposite direction of the blue nun.

Joslin returned with her mirror a moment later.

"Where did Yuri go?" she asked, feeling a bit miffed that he had left without her.

"Oh, he had better things to do," Elissa told her.

"Huh?" she answered, ruefully staring at the emptiness in the long corridor.

"It is all about keeping your balance," Elissa quipped. Then she abruptly changed the subject. "You know, Arcas drew a great likeness of my great Aunt Nemesis."

"What?" Joslin questioned. She quickly quit staring at the vacant corridor and swung around toward Elissa, who continued to reminiscence over the pictures. She held the mirror opposite Arcas's cryptic handwriting and began reading the note out loud. "Dear Joslin, hopefully by now you have found the room of radioactive debris. It contains the remnants of a nuclear fission attack wrought by the Serpentines forty-thousand years ago. Please, do not panic, but we are under a nuclear threat now. Remember to potentize the rocks before using them therapeutically. Love, Dad."

"Good job, dear," Elissa commented. "I knew that you could pull it together."

"How do you potentize?" Joslin asked as she lifted the mirror again against the note. "Oh, here is a PS. It says to ask my dragon."

"That's no problem," Elissa insisted. "I can help you with the potentizing. Let's get back to the pictures."

Stunned, Joslin slowly nodded her consent.

"Once upon a time," Elissa began, "there was an evil Serpentine Federation that scared the universe to death with the threat of their nuclear weapons. They lived off of souls who feared the worst. They blasted away several star civilizations and pursued the refugees to the planet Earth, which was made only in seven days under duress. They had a difficult time getting a strong foothold on the planet until the intergalactic wars, where they spliced into the gene pool of captured humans in ancient Egypt. They were stopped only by a group of transparent dragons that had escorted the Yeti refugees from Draco. You can see why the Yeti are so good at hiding. The Yeti came after the Anasazi had stabilized the planet. The dragon escorts transmuted the radiation from the Serpentine attack and learned how to conceal themselves. This is how everyone escaped undetected by the reptilian-brained-only Serpentines.

"Life is too simple for a reptilian-brained-only type," Elissa added as a side note. Then she continued reading. "Your dragon can show you how to transmute the energy of this last nuclear attack and heal the wasteland."

Joslin shrugged at her dragon.

"Now let's go fetch some radioactive rocks and potentize them," Elissa suggested. "Gerwyn can give the antidote to the blue nun to use on the Marlboro wasteland. This is how we reclaim Pellinor's nuked property and cede it as our own. His heirs are wasted on a Grail quest and will not ever return."

Joslin hurried into the rooms of radioactive rock and made remedies for the blue nun. She met with the woman and sent her back to Wales with a mission. The transparent dragons could help the nuns get to their destinies without being detected. The wasted heirs of Pellinor would notice them only as a dream and would not pose a threat.

"Great job, that's my queen," Elissa encouraged after Joslin had completed her assignment. "Just one more history lesson before you can get back to Yuri, who is holding a concert at the other end of the library."

Joslin sat down on the floor of the corridor and caught her breath.

Elissa continued, "Lancelot became the first Grail knight. It was his karma because he had been John the Baptist in a previous incarnation. It was his job to guard the Grail that Joseph of Arimathea had retrieved with his son

Josephus. His other son, James the Just, died with the others crucified with Jesse. They did not want Jesse's cup to fall into the hands of Roman soldiers, who would exploit its healing powers. Unfortunately, Maury the Knight had a sister named Guinevere, who seduced Lancelot and gave the Grail to the Roman clergy. Another knight named Perceval seized the Grail from the bishop and gave it back to Joseph of Arimathea."

"Is it the same one that lies at the bottom of the well at Glastonbury?" Joslin asked. She recalled that Maury the Knight had also been the Queen of England. Queen Maury and Joslin's father had died while battling the bishop near the Marlboro Castle. Her father had been king of the United Kingdoms, which included England.

"Yes, it is the same Holy Grail that Joseph of Arimathea threw when he became upset at Pellinor. Pellinor, his great-grandson, flipped out after his first wife died. He did not want the Grail falling into the wrong hands, after King Mark imprisoned James's family in Londinium. King Mark, the son of Salome, patronized Mary of Magdelene and profited from destroying James's position with the Council of Jerusalem. King Mark sought to resurrect the ancient Egyptian court that had attacked Boudica, after she helped Joseph of Arimathea escape. Joseph of Arimathea knew that the Serpentine Romans and their clergy would not look for the Grail in a well. They are only linear thinkers."

"Got it," Joslin commented with a yawn. "Lancelot partnered with the niece of the Fisher King, who had already lost his land to the Roman soldiers. She died on a Dragon flying mission while their son, Galahad, was very small. Galahad was the nephew of Mother Superior, who taught him about Stonehenge."

"It always helps to know your history," Elissa told Joslin, before adding, "That's all for now. Sleep in."

Chapter Eighteen

The lively art of

Washing away tragedies

That have run their course

Tune Reference: *Take Me To The River*

----Talking Heads

"LET'S GET BACK to our cave at Lake Hovsgol," Joslin announced the next morning.

Yuri rolled out of bed as he stretched and yawned. "It will be great to get out in the sunshine again."

Joslin sat up in bed, beaming happiness and contentment. After savoring the first major decision that she felt confident about in the past several weeks, another thought flashed across her mind and her countenance grew serious. "Ohhh, I almost forgot about the nestlings."

"Ohhh, that one is easy," Yuri replied. He stood in front of her and began dressing for the move back to the cave. Tossing on his tunic, he said lightly, "The same Dragon flyers that transported the nuns can finish bringing the nestlings. Smoke can come with us to the cave. He makes a great babysitter."

Joslin laughed and lay back down. After pausing briefly to savor the relaxing moment, she resolutely rose from her bed. Hurriedly dressing and packing at the same time, she joined Yuri, who was heading out the door.

"I'll help Gerwyn pack up Smoke and the others. I'll summon the Siberian Dragon flyers through the crystal mineral network," Yuri told her and then kissed her on the forehead. Then his eyes twinkled and he said, "Go get some breakfast. You were up late last night."

Joslin chuckled, running off to attend to other matters before breakfast. Turning and waving at her husband, she announced, "Meet me at the cave by lunch."

At lunchtime, the entire family, including Smoke, gathered in the cave's kitchen. Smoke busily blew intermittent puffs of smoke, temporarily illuminating the outline of his sleek, shimmering body. He continued to mesmerize Gerwyn at the table, and Joslin and Yuri sat down on the benches across from each other. Joslin produced the diamond crystal that Patrick had given her and placed it on the table. She stared into the different facets of the diamond and sipped her herb tea.

"It is my understanding that the first people to inhabit earth were the Neanderthals from the star system Draco," she began.

"That is what my father told me," Yuri agreed. "They came about two-hundred-million years ago. The human form came into existence eight-million years ago. The celestial refugees in Draco eventually concluded that a form unique to the new planet would be required. The Serpentines would not be able to distinguish refugees from the various star systems if everyone had the same form. When the human form became established, the star seed civilizations arrived. Unfortunately, the Serpentines had already infiltrated the ranks of the human form, which they destroyed in a global flood. The flood occurred about four-million years ago. The Pleiadians came to help stabilize the planet during all the changes. They adopted the human form and became the Anasazi, inhabiting the planet for a little less than a million years. Then they ascended after the intergalactic wars of ancient Egypt."

"My father told me that there were three major civilizations on the planet before the intergalactic wars," Joslin remembered. "One group consisted of the Neanderthals, the second group was the Anasazi, and the third civilization was called Atlantis. Atlantis was formed eight-hundred-thousand years ago, and it sank forty-thousand years ago."

"That puts everything into perspective," Yuri observed.

Joslin smirked. "From a geologic standpoint, our time on this planet is just a drop in the bucket."

"Time is speeding up," Yuri noted. "Things happen in hundreds of years now rather than millions of years."

"You're right, Yuri," Joslin agreed. "I never considered the rate of growth to be exponential."

"I think Mom called it a learning curve." Yuri smiled. His mother had partnered with a Neanderthal. "Though some things, like Dad, don't change much through the years."

"That's what makes him so special." Joslin sighed. "There is a lot to be said for consistency."

"Hey, Mom, that's quite a rock you've got there. It is almost like the one in the picture," Gerwyn interrupted.

"What picture?" Joslin asked, quickly turning her attention to her young son.

"The one on the wall near the rock rooms," he said as he pointed his small finger at the rock. "It goes on top of the pyramid."

"The pyramid of Cheops?" Yuri questioned with a quizzical glance at Joslin.

Joslin scooped Gerwyn into her arms. She hugged him and planted several soft kisses on the top of his head. He delightedly wiggled in her lap.

"Elissa told me about Cheops," he replied.

"Thank heavens for Elissa!" Joslin exclaimed. "She saved us a trip back to the library."

"She said that the Serpentines took out the top," Gerwyn continued as he looked up at both of his parents. "It happened during the intergalactic wars of ancient Egypt."

"Did she say how they recovered diamond crystal?" Joslin questioned.

"No, she didn't," Gerwyn answered. He appeared slightly confused for a moment but quickly went on to another topic. "Smoke wants to go outside and practice puffing. He said that he needs my help."

"Oh." Yuri looked thoughtful for a moment and then said, "Go entertain Smoke. Your mother and I will solve this latest mystery."

Gerwyn stepped down from his mother's lap and ran out of the cave with Smoke. Joslin rose from the table and Yuri joined her. They headed for the Dragon stalls at the other end of the cave.

"What happened to the diamond crystal at the top of Cheops pyramid?" Joslin asked when they found the golden Sea Dragon queen.

"It fell to the ground during the Serpentine attack," Elissa replied. "The Serpentines forgot to remove it first. They have a one-track mind, you know. They became so enthralled with their pyrotechnics that they overlooked a critical detail."

"How critical was the detail?" Joslin asked.

"Well, planet Earth won the war as a result," she answered, preening the dirt from her scaled fingers. "The diamond crystal has a magnetic quality that returns it to earth."

"Who found it? And how did it decisively win the war?" Joslin quizzed.

"A temple priestess retrieved the diamond crystal from the ground," Elissa explained. "She placed it inside a pre-made grid system that ejected the intruders from the planet. They all left in one big swoop. The entire area had been under strict surveillance, and she could not reach it without being observed. She had been waiting for the Serpentines' attack to get the crystal. The priestess knew that they would miss it completely."

"Keep going," Elissa encouraged.

"The priestess caught it in a glove designed to attract it. It was a magnetic attraction. Unfortunately, it wasn't strong enough to pull the diamond crystal from the mortar at the top, and she had to wait for it to drop in freefall."

"Why isn't it in the grid now?" Joslin asked.

"Infiltrators removed it," Elissa said, switching hands to clean the nails on the other side of her body.

"And somehow Patrick managed to obtain it?" Joslin persisted.

"Yes, long story," Elissa answered as she examined her appearance in a mirror. "Later. Now go frolic. Remember to keep the balance in life."

Chapter Nineteen

The lively art of

Being mesmerized by movement

To get back in the flow

Tune Reference: *Chasing Cars*

----Snow Patrol

"HUMPH," JOSLIN REMARKED as she and Yuri left the Dragon stalls. "Thrown out of the cave by my own Sea Dragon."

"She said to frolic," Yuri reminded her with a hint teasing in his voice. "Someone has got to keep the queen happy."

Joslin couldn't keep from laughing when she heard his words. After a brief moment of hysterics, she suggested, "I could use a long soak in the hot springs now. Do you think that we could sneak back to Utopia unannounced?"

"I'm sure that I could arrange to have one of my buddies reserve a private section for us," Yuri quietly said. "Ivan could take us to the garden hot springs and back. Wear your invisible armor and the others will think that I've come alone to retrieve supplies. You'll have to stay close to me. That way they won't notice you."

Joslin agreed to the plan. Moments later, the happy couple entered the garden in Utopia. Joslin removed her clothes and slowly slipped inside the warm blue pool. Remembering the first time she saw Elissa glittering in the pool, she stopped to retrieve the diamond crystal. Holding it close to the surface of the pool, she noticed the patterns of light reflecting off the stone walls of the cavern. The diamond had been cut in a certain manner to reveal a story within. Like the story depicted on the walls of the Rhakotis corridor, another series of pictures reflected from the diamond crystal.

Immediately Joslin understood the significance of the crystal reflections. She felt awed by the sight and sat mesmerized in the pool of water. Staring at the spectacle filling the cavern, she calmly accepted Yuri's light kisses on her neck and shoulders. The ambiance dulled her mind, and she responded to his overtures. Afterward, she drifted into a light sleep beside him on the warm bank.

The reflections on the walls of the cavern swirled in her head. She dreamed scenerios that she knew but could not remember. When she awoke, she gazed silently at the designs around her and realized that the priestess had gridded the diamond crystals with the Four Directions. Recalling that the Native Americans from the Spica star system used the Four Directions, she understood that the theme pertained to her next destination. After kissing Yuri's cheek lightly, she slipped back into the luminous blue pool.

Without any further discussion, the couple left Utopia after indulging in one last brief swim. They both were still thinking over the patterns they saw through the reflections of the diamond crystal. Joslin pursued the immediate task of returning the diamond crystal to a grid in the Four Directions. She reserved her questions about the history of the diamond crystal until she fully understood what she had seen on the ceiling above the luminous blue pool.

"We need to restore the diamond crystal in a grid consisting of the Four Directions," Joslin told Elissa the following day as the golden Dragon's caretaker applied the finishing touches to her grooming. Elissa appeared very shiny and refreshed in the early morning sunlight.

"Seems that you and Yuri viewed the reflection within the diamond crystal," Elissa observed with a dainty toss of her golden head.

"Yes, I am still fathoming the meaning of the pattern in my dreams," Joslin answered.

"Don't dream about it too much," the golden Sea Dragon queen said. "You might get lost."

"I know. There is that attraction," Joslin said. "It becomes too easy to escape into a fantasy given the present circumstances."

"I know," Elissa said. "The history of the world is overwhelming. So KISS: Keep It Simple."

Joslin asked hurriedly. "So how do we make it simple?"

"Find the original grid with the Four Directions," Elissa replied.

Throwing her hands up in the air with a slight sense of hopelessness, Joslin questioned, "Where do we start?"

"You are tired," she told Joslin. "This is something you could have figured out yourself, at least how to start."

"I know," she admitted. "It isn't easy getting closer to someone."

Elissa chuckled. "I know. It only took a little less than eight hundred thousand years for me to shack up with Ivan. It is time that we learn our lessons through joy."

"There's perspective for you," Joslin commented. "I think that I will start with my own grid for the Four Directions and track the energy."

"There's a start." Elissa smiled. "Let me know when you are ready to go find it."

Joslin left the Sea Dragon to her grooming and wandered to a ledge overlooking Lake Hovsgol. She collected several stones and objects that attracted her and placed them in a pattern. There was a stone in the center with others marking the directions of north, east, south, and west. She studied the arrangement, sensing the energy of the sacred wheel. A flash of insight prompted her to replace the center stone with the diamond crystal. Immediately she realized where she could find the original grid from ancient Egypt. She removed the diamond crystal from the center and reinserted the other stone. Leaving the grid where it stood on the cliff, she raced back to Elissa.

"You and I are going to Tibet," she announced to the Sea Dragon queen.

Elissa smiled as she thought about Joslin's proposal. "You're right. Let's go now."

Chapter Twenty

Some things are
Worth remembering

Tune Reference: *Longer*
----Dan Folgelberg

"WAIT A MOMENT," Joslin cautioned Elissa. "We gotta slow down. I need to know where to go in Tibet. I need to get past the Serpentines who overtook Shambala. I need to let Yuri and Gerwyn know that I am leaving on a mission."

"You need to relax," Elissa suggested. "Think about it. I think that Yuri, even Gerwyn, can help with this one."

"How?" Joslin questioned, already donning her invisible armor.

"Think about it. Or go ask Yuri. I bet he knows where it is and I bet that he knows how to get there safely."

"Who?" Joslin asked, shaking her head. She seemed perplexed by Elissa's advice. She gently accused her Sea Dragon, "You are being a mystery."

"You are confusing the issue," Elissa retorted softly. "You aren't even pregnant or postpartum. It is not the hormones; it's the honeymoon. I am being the wise one in this pair of us."

"You're right," Joslin thoughtfully said. "It's the honeymoon. You can see why I got pregnant first. It was easier."

"All right then. Now that we have our little understanding, I suggest that you follow up with Yuri but not in the manner that you initially thought," Elissa coached.

"Right," Joslin said, turning toward the cave with a deep breath.

She marched to the suite where she knew that she could find Yuri playing with Gerwyn. The young men laughed and giggled as Smoke appeared in different locations in the area. Gerwyn ran toward his transparent dragon and hugged him. "Daddy is helping me play hide and go seek with Smoke," Gerwyn informed his mom.

"Gerwyn does the seeking and Smoke does the hiding," Yuri explained.

"I have a question for the three of you," Joslin ventured.

Both Yuri and Gerwyn looked at Joslin eagerly. Smoke puffed away, his fading appearance taking his attentive grin with it. Joslin surveyed the threesome, noting their eagerness to help.

"Where do you think I would find the Four Directions grid from ancient Egypt?" Joslin asked.

"Singing Cave," Yuri offered.

"Yes, Singing Cave," Gerwyn and Smoke agreed. "Mommy, you can borrow my singer crystal to find it. You go through the MidEarth."

"Huh!" Joslin murmured, shaking her head with slight disbelief. Relaxing finally, she gave the threesome a group hug.

"Smoke showed me while we were on one of our adventures," Gerwyn explained.

Yuri shrugged and nodded. "I thought that it was a great idea as long as they were home the next day."

"Where was I?" Joslin questioned, trying to remember the occasion.

"In Wales," Gerwyn piped.

"OK," Joslin acquiesced as she kissed them all. "Let's make a picnic out of it."

"Start packing," Yuri encouraged the youngsters as Gerwyn and Smoke excitedly left to collect their things.

The young family left with their dragons for the portal to the MidEarth through Utopia. They entered the portal undetected by the inhabitants in the same secretive manner that the couple had visited the hot springs. Moments later, they were flying through the air of the MidEarth.

"Mom, look! Smoke is visible now!" Gerwyn cried with delight.

"Nothing like flying in the MidEarth to bring out a person's true colors," Yuri happily replied, answering for Joslin.

Smoke appeared very handsome in the rarified atmosphere. Gerwyn directed them toward the tunnel that led to Singing Cave. Joslin and Elissa followed closely behind the others. She could hear an invigorating *om* emanating from the recesses of the MidEarth.

"Look, Mom!" Gerwyn shouted. "There's the grid for the diamond crystal."

One hundred meters from Singing Cave's opening to the outside world, Joslin spotted the grid for the Four Directions embedded into the bedrock.

"This is it," she responded as she examined the arrangement. "Great job, Gerwyn and Smoke."

After Elissa landed near the arrangement, she kneeled and inserted the clear diamond crystal in the center of the Four Directions. The diameter of the clear crystal diamond was exactly twelve centimeters. Though it was a diamond in the rough, it fit perfectly inside the groove. Immediately, the same pattern on the wall of the hot springs appeared on the walls of the rocky tavern. This time, the colors in the patterns were intensified and the locations of the rest of the diamond crystals could be determined.

Yuri gazed at the pictures on the wall and began his interpretation. "The clear diamond crystal in the center is universal. The picture on the walls depicts the zodiac and related constellations. We have four more diamonds in the rough to find. There are pre-made grooves for each of them."

"It is beautiful, Mom," Gerwyn commented. Then he added, "See, you do not have to do this alone."

Joslin smiled at her son's remarks as Yuri put his arm around her with a gentle squeeze for emphasis.

"Got it," she replied as a small tear trickled down her cheek. "It is much, much easier with all of your help. Thank you."

"There are four other diamonds in the rough," Yuri continued. "The blue one is in India along the Narmada River. The yellow diamond can be found in Britain. The green diamond is located in India, again, in the Indus Valley. Our friends from the Noris star system are guarding it in their Dragon temple."

"That one will be easy," Joslin remarked with some mild relief.

"Relatively," Yuri replied with a quick glance in her direction.

"The last diamond is brown," Gerwyn continued, picking up where his father had dropped off. "It is located in the Himalayas near Utopia, but it is not in the Altai Mountain range. Good luck with this one, Mom."

"One is a start," she answered, remembering to stay positive in the face of her son's hard, steely logic, typical of his maturation age.

"Great job, everyone," Yuri encouraged with heartfelt enthusiasm, before casting a sideways glance at his partner concerning parenting issues.

Joslin caught his eye and nodded assuredly. "OK, we will do this all together. I got the message. Meanwhile, I'll put someone on this planetarium right away. It will take at least a year for a pictograph expert to grasp the meaning of all these patterns and meanings. The visions are very rich. It will take more than a year to obtain their meanings. There are several important visions linked to some of the zodiac designs. They have important information."

Yuri nodded with an anxious look on his face. One of the visions associated with a particular zodiac design disturbed him. Joslin noticed his concerned expression, and briefly studied the arrangement.

After a brief second of hesitation, she decided, "Let's head back to Utopia before we are tracked."

They quickly left the tunnel and soared over the MidEarth. When they had passed into Utopia, Joslin asked McGrail, Gilderoy's caretaker, to decipher the images depicted in the planetarium. Gilderoy appeared delighted to help with this mission.

Chapter Twenty-One

The power of the stars

Is guidance

Tune Reference: Aquarius/*Let The Sunshine In (The Flesh Failures)*
[From the American Tribal Love Rock Musical "Hair"]
----The Fifth Dimension

"WE ARE GOING for the green diamond first," Joslin announced after they had rested a day at Lake Hovsgol.

"That's the one that goes in the east," Gerwyn stated.

"Yes, that is correct," Yuri recalled slowly.

"Let's leave tomorrow early in the morning," Joslin said. It will be easier to outrun the Serpentine Dragons in the Gobi Desert in daylight. Their personal habits are nocturnal."

They landed uneventfully in the Valley of the Indus. A crowd of Hindoo disciples gathered around them and escorted them to the temple that housed the White-eared dragons. Joslin noticed how green and fertile the valley appeared.

"Hello," Ferndale, the smaller White-eared dragon of the three, greeted them.

"How's the rain making?" Joslin asked. "The valley is beautiful."

"We have the system down," a Hindoo disciple answered. "We take care of Ferndale and his buddies. Ferndale condenses the snow for us with his dragon breath. The rains come, and we get to keep our crops."

"I hear that you came for the green crystal diamond," Charles interrupted, getting straight to the point. Charles was Ferndale's older brother.

"Yes," Joslin responded. "The planetarium indicated that we could find it here."

"Mighty Moe has been guarding it," Charles answered. "He has been watching the fire reflected inside it. It suddenly became stronger a few days ago. We sensed that you had found the clear-crystal diamond and placed it in its appropriate grid."

"Sounds like you knew more about what was going on than we did," Joslin observed. "I feel as if I am on a scavenger hunt."

"You are," Charles said dryly.

"Can you tell us more about the green-crystal diamond?" Joslin asked. "Why are the crystal diamonds scattered over Eurasia?"

"I can tell you what I know," Charles replied. "First, let's get the crystal from Mighty Moe, though I prefer to let sleeping dragons lie, if you know what I mean. However, the presence of the green-crystal diamond may elucidate the matter." Charles paused before continuing. "I have a great idea. We'll just sound the dinner bell and offer Mighty Moe a snack. That will rouse him from his slumber."

Joslin heard the gong sound off. From the recesses of the temple, a huge, bright red Sea Dragon emerged. He sauntered over to his brother Charles.

"I heard you," he told his older brother as he handed the green-crystal diamond over to Joslin. "Do you believe that I only think about my stomach? I knew that she was here all along. I just wanted to hear the gong."

"Mighty Moe is also a musician," Charles explained before he and Mighty Moe began rolling on the floor of the temple in a playful wrestle. "Trying to pull a fast one on me, huh, little brother!"

Joslin told Yuri and Gerwyn, "Let's step outside while these two play. On second thought, let's just take off. I have a feeling that we will learn more by just placing it inside the grid and studying the reflected pattern."

Yuri stared at the twelve-centimeter crystal in her hands. He agreed, "The same thought crossed my mind. I prefer to let lying dragons play."

The young familyquickly assembled around the Four Directions grid in Singing Cave. Joslin placed the green-crystal diamond in the groove and new patterns emerged in the reflections on the walls. One particular pattern caught Joslin's eye immediately.

"The green-diamond crystal is from Alpha Centauri, which is the former star system of the Noris. Some went east and settled in the Indus Valley," she remarked. "A Pegasus removed it from the Four Directions grid when my great-grandfather King Cole died."

"In the history of the world, that is fairly recent," Yuri observed. "It appears that the green diamond stabilized the situation in the Indus Valley."

"Yes, King Cole died mysteriously during a visit to Pellinor," Joslin added. "They found his body in a forest near the Tintagel Castle. Nobody could determine the cause of death. He founded Camelon, building it after the Iceni fled Camulodunum. The Roman Serpentines had rebuilt Camulodunum after his grandmother Boudica's rebellion ended suddenly. She acended to avoid capture and Druidic Dragon flyers airlifted the remaining tribe members. After Constantinople killed King Cole's successor, my father Arcas, they renamed the town Colchester."

"Keep going," Yuri encouraged.

"King Cole's grandfather, Boudica's partner, led the Noris, or Norfolk from the Iceland area. They eventually settled in eastern England after the Serpentines attacked their northern sod villages. The Druids called them Iceni because they came directly from Iceland. They partnered with the Arctos, who also had escaped the Serpentine attacks in Siberia. Some Arctos escaped to the west and intermarried with the Celtics. Boudica descended from these Celtic refugees, or displaced Atlanteans. These Atlanteans had anticipated that a meteorite would strike Atlantis and sought higher ground. After the sinking of Atlantis by Lemurian insurgents, the Grays came and built a base off the island where someone found the green diamond. Called Greenland, the island had been the site where the Noris first landed on the planet. The metamorphosis of a rock underneath their first landing platform formed the green diamond, which came to represent their stake in the new planet. The reflections from the flame of the green diamond illustrate the history of the Alpha Centauri star system as well as the exodus of the Noris."

"My Neanderthal ancestors helped the Atlanteans settle in the Siberian and Himalayan caves," Yuri commented. "My father told me about it."

"They also assisted the Noris when they landed in Greenland," Joslin added. "Kuan Yin studied the Noris principles of balance and harmony at the temple in the Valley of the Indus. According to the inscriptions reflected here, she was the time traveler who brought the green diamond to the temple after King Cole died. It had something to do with the time wrinkle that my dad created that time. Returning the crystal diamonds to the Four-Directions grid retrieves some vital links pertaining to that particular time wrinkle."

"It apparently protects us from those intergalactic forces that invaded ancient Egypt," Yuri observed. "The crystal energetically ties the four compass directions together in a manner that blocks whatever doesn't possess the planet's magnetic attraction."

"The aliens from ancient Egypt—like the Serpentines, Sirius's Black Dogs, Grays, and Vega's Blues—lack a carbon base in their DNA as well as magnetite in their skulls," Joslin explained. "They could not intuitively tell you the direction of magnetic north because they lack a sense of direction. They do not have an internal compass and exist without a spiritual connection to the planet, which has been cultivated in the human form by their own choice over time."

"Those humans who choose to ignore their intuition, sense of balance, and sense of connection with the natural world become disconnected eventually," Yuri continued. "This is why Pellinor became vulnerable to Serpentine attack."

"It is the aftermath of Armageddon, which occurred on the plains surrounding the Castle Marlboro," Joslin said. "The division between good and evil is becoming wider and wider."

"Love keeps the planet rotating," Yuri reflected. He stood, awestruck, underneath the planetarium inside the walls of the Singing Cave.

"The fall of Atlantis concerned the mind's true liberation," Joslin rejoined. "The inhabitants of the planet must be guided by peace rather than traumatic exodus."

Chapter Twenty-Two

Why did Christ runaway?

Tune Reference: *Southern Cross*

----Crosby, Stills, and Nash

"LOOK, MOM AND Dad!" Gerwyn shouted, who until then had remained quiet throughout the retrieval of the green-crystal diamond. "I see a new constellation over there."

"You're right, Gerwyn!" his father replied with enthusiasm. "Sharp eye."

"It's a Southern Cross, like the Four-Directions grid," Joslin observed in wonder.

"Hmmm." Yuri pondered the riddle, and then his eyes brightened with awareness. "It lies in the southern hemisphere of the sky."

"Its appearance has something to do with our mission now," Joslin interrupted. "I think the significance will become clearer after we retrieve the yellow-crystal diamond in London. We can find it at the Roman temple that the Saxons converted into a Druidic Christian church. All these crystal diamonds for the Four-Directions grid have been relocated to sacred places. A priestess set up the London grid."

"She maintained the sacred tradition," Yuri commented.

They spent the night camping around the Four-Directions grid, and the next morning they set off for London. Landing near a church on the outskirts of town. the family met several of Joslin's Saxon cousins, who came to greet her.

"I hear that you came for the yellow crystal diamond. I dreamed about it last night," a priest explained as he showed them where they could board the Sea Dragons.

"How did it get here?" Yuri asked one of his assistants.

"Joseph of Arimathea brought it after he threw the Holy Grail in the well," the assistant answered. "They killed Joseph of Arimathea a few days later. This occurred shortly before your father was born."

"What happened to the yellow-crystal diamond?" Joslin questioned.

"It had been given to the Serpentine Dragons to guard in the temple," the priest replied. "We recovered it when we razed London. Here, take it."

The priest produced the yellow-crystal diamond from underneath his cloak. He handed it to Joslin as he said, "The yellow crystal served as a Trojan horse."

Joslin appeared perplexed. Yuri shrugged and Gerwyn cocked his head from side to side. The Saxons smiled when they noticed their confusion. "What do you mean?" Joslin demanded, weighing the stone in her hands.

"The stone was formed when the Serpentines attacked Pleiades," the priest began. "A rock underneath their most popular sacred site metamorphosed. The Anasazi brought it with them and used the rock in a grid to stabilize the planet during intense change. Joseph of Arimathea knew that the yellow-crystal diamond could be used to summon help from the other side, especially those who the Serpentines martyred."

"So martyrdom is not a sanctioned rite of passage," Joslin surmised. "It just enables the soul to return more powerful from another dimension."

"With certain caveats," the priest explained. "The reality is that a true martyr never really gives up. It is just another way to best a competitor, in this case the Serpentines. The Southern Cross pertains to three major portals. One portal leads to the sacred site on the Pleiades where the celestials were martyred. A second portal goes to a dimension where the early Christian martyrs escaped. The third portal pertains to the martyrs that died when the Serpentine Federation destroyed Lemuria. Placing the yellow crystal in the Four-Directions grid will reveal the endpoints of these portals. You must visit them in the southern hemisphere; otherwise the yellow-crystal diamond will not be stable in the grid. That is one reason why the Four-Directions grid in Singing Cave could be quickly dismantled. It became unstable with the evolution of events on the planet."

"The placement of the yellow-crystal diamond in the Londinium Temple was a foot in the door for these so-called returning martyrs," another assistant added. "They left in a sacred manner and they returned empowered in the sacred. This time they drove the Serpentines out of the area."

"It is a very ruthless technique," Yuri commented.

"Yes, but it worked." The priest shrugged. "There are always those who choose not to be victims, even on their dying day."

"It is a function of spirit, which their enemies lack," a third assistant explained in a feminine voice. "Enemies such as the Serpentines, Grays, Black Dogs, or Blues either have no spirit or possess a degenerated one. They must rely on instinctual needs for motivation."

Joslin turned toward the woman's voice. The figure remained hidden behind the masculine cloak, and Joslin did not press further. Though Joslin's vision enabled her to visualize the woman behind the cloth, she honored the use of discretion.

The priest drew Joslin aside and whispered, "Though we won here and the situation is stabilized, there are remnants of the former ruling order that still threaten our freedoms. Until these remnants fully understand what it is like to be free, it is prudent to choose our battles so that we do not scatter our energy."

Joslin nodded softly. Then she said, "Thank you for saving me a visit to the former site of the Londinium Temple. We must leave now."

"One last thing," Yuri interjected. "If Joseph of Arimathea had just given the stone to the Londinium Temple, would they have accepted it?"

"Probably not," the priest said in a regular voice. "He anticipated that they would kill him for it. When they gave the stone a position of honor in the temple, he considered his mission a posthumous success."

"That is what I figured," Yuri responded as he ushered Gerwyn in the direction of their Sea Dragons. "I just wanted to be sure of this small detail, which is incredibly significant."

The eyes of the priest glistened. He acknowledged Yuri's understanding with a smile and a nod. The assistants stood aside as the family retrieved their dragons and flew away in the London fog.

When they reached the Singing Cave, Joslin rushed to the Four-Directions grid and placed the yellow-crystal diamond in the groove. More patterns and script emerged on the walls of the planetarium. Gerwyn unraveled his bedroll on the floor of the cave and lay down to gaze at the reflected visions, which were almost as peacefully illuminating as a real night sky.

"It's pretty, Mom and Dad," he said thoughtfully.

Moments later, he fell asleep on top of his bedroll. Yuri placed a blanket over him and arranged his bedroll next to Joslin's. Then he reclined on the floor and motioned for Joslin. She sat down on their joined bedrolls. She planted a soft kiss on his cheek as he put his arm around her. Together they stared, dumbfounded, at the walls of the cave.

"It is amazing what a person can get by just inner reflections," Joslin remarked. "Who would have guessed all this was inside of those diamonds in the rough."

"Looks like we are going to New Zealand tomorrow." Yuri grinned wryly as he lay down on his bedroll. "The Senoi will be happy to see you."

"Me?" She nudged him, teasing him gently.

"You're the one with the yellow crystal diamond." He smiled. "I just get to step back and rest. I wonder what they have to trade in New Zealand?"

Joslin lay down on her bedroll with a chuckle. "I'm sure they'll give you a great bargain for your metal weapons."

She soon fell asleep. This night she dreamed about the portals. Sometimes they became hot and sometimes they were cold. She dreamed of aborigines and odd birds dressed in black capes and white tunics. In the morning, they quietly ventured through the first portal and met the inhabitants at the other end. Elissa and Ivan served as interpreters for the two groups of people.

"We dreamed about your coming last night," the New Zealanders told her. "We want to work with you."

"Great," Joslin told them. "Tell us about your dreams with the yellow diamond."

"That's easy," the Senoi chieftain replied. "We discussed our dreams at the community hut this morning. Everyone saw the yellow-crystal diamond. It represents our link to the universal soul. We are the spiritual warriors or guardians of this soul. We will first protect the earth in our dreams, which will eventually play out in the mundane."

"Thank you for watching out for all of us," Joslin acknowledged. "We will send emissaries through the portal to maintain the connection."

"Thank you for keeping us updated," the chieftain replied. "I know that you have been busy. We see it in our dreams."

Then the family left for the next portal. For the moment, Yuri decided against promoting commerce with the tribes. The validation of the cosmic danger from far corners of the world unnerved him. The dreams were real.

The next portal took them to the Stirling Range in western Australia. The aborigines at the end of the portal greeted Joslin and handed her a bouquet of white flowers. Joslin inhaled their aroma before sharing it with Yuri and Gerwyn.

"The Latin name for the flowers is *Xanthosia rotundifolia*, otherwise known as southern cross," Elissa said.

"They even have a flower for the constellation!" Joslin exclaimed with delight.

"Yes," the aborigine woman who had handed her the bouquet answered. "It only takes one whiff to know that your thoughts create your reality."

"I believe it," Yuri said as he handed the bouquet of southern crosses back to Joslin.

"Positive thoughts for a positive outcome," Joslin acknowledged. "Thank you for this flower of enlightenment."

"Let's see the yellow-crystal diamond," a tall aborigine man said.

"Oh look, the stone reminds me of the flower's center," the aborigine woman observed. "You can imagine it in the fire within the rock."

"Some call it a mandala," Elissa added. "It helps center your soul."

"Looks like we can find some great tools for inspiration here," Joslin said. "We will send emissaries through this portal to maintain this important connection. Thank you so much for being there."

"You are welcome," the collection of Australian aborigines replied in chorus. "Keep us updated."

The family hurried on to the third portal. This one led to Antarctica. A flock of penguins surrounded them at the endpoint.

"These are the birds that I dreamed of last night!" Gerwyn shouted, pointing at the dignified birds wobbling around the snowy terrain. The penguins moved in closer. Some baby birds peered at them from underneath the wings of their parents. Yuri glanced down at Gerwyn, who was hiding behind his legs.

"They are reflections of us!" He laughed. "They were in my dreams too."

"Mine too." Joslin also laughed, studying the birds around her. "They are all dressed up and have nowhere to go. Their short wings make flying impossible. These birds, like dreams, take us many places without ever going anywhere."

"Look, they slide around in the snow like they are flying. They even swim in and out of the water," Gerwyn observed with astonishment. "They know how to have fun. They don't need to go anywhere."

Both Yuri and Joslin chuckled at Gerwyn's observations. The antics of the penguins amused them. Their short, furry feathers reminded Joslin of the birds in her dream with black capes and white tunics. She produced the yellow-crystal diamond from the pocket of her own cloak and displayed it in the palm of her hand. Inside the stone, she could see the reflection of the merry birds against the clear white background.

"This portal is about lucid dreaming and astral projection," she said. "It elucidates the connection between the dream state and the awakened life."

"You know, the penguins' dress reminds me of Mother Superior's habit," Yuri commented. "They are very inspiring creatures. Both inhabit isolated regions of mind and space like our wandering mystics in Australia."

"Let's get back to Singing Cave and make a fire," Gerwyn urged. "It's freezing out here. If this is a dream, I don't want to stay in it too long."

"Great point," Yuri acknowledged.

One of the larger penguins waddled toward Joslin's extended palm and touched his reflection inside the diamond crystal. Then he looked up at Joslin and quickly backed away. Joslin smiled and tucked the stone away inside her cloak.

"I think that he is telling us to stay focused," she surmised. "I agree. Let's go."

They raced back to the Singing Cave, where the caretakers had made a small bonfire. A light draft carried the smoke out of the cave, allowing the family to warm themselves by the fire without losing sight of the Four-Directions grid. After she had sensation inside the tips of her cold fingers again, Joslin reinserted the yellow-crystal diamond. They continued to gaze at the patterns on the wall as they ate their supper. When they finished, they fell asleep on their bedrolls and slipped back into their dreams.

Chapter Twenty-Three

The lively art of

Absolutes

As a check on reality

Tune Reference: *Apologize*

----OneRepublic

JOSLIN AWOKE AND sat up on her bedroll. She watched the rest of the members of her family slowly stir. They noticed that she was already awake and smiled when they fully opened their eyes.

"We are going for the brown-crystal diamond today," she quietly told them with confidence. "It is in the Himalayas."

Yuri quickly rolled over and began preparing for the trip. "We must have had the same dream."

Gerwyn awoke much slower, fighting the tendency to roll over and go back to sleep. Eventually, curiosity got the better of him. He rose and ran over to kiss his mother good morning. Joslin stood and they prepared breakfast together.

"Where in the Himalayas are we going?" Gerwyn asked. "It wasn't clear on the diagrams."

"The color of the crystal diamond is brown. It fits in the southern position of the Four-Directions grid and relates to the element of fire," she began. "I suspect that we are heading toward a volcano or hot spot in the Himalayas."

"It looks like we will be visiting your grandfather," Yuri told Gerwyn, and he kissed his family. Then he sat down at the kitchen table and began eating his breakfast.

"Huh?" Joslin questioned, joining him at the table.

"See, the map points to his stomping grounds," Yuri said. "By the way, there are no volcanoes in Tibet, though the mountains are the result of intense volcanic activity."

"Volcanoes build mountains." Joslin suggested. "Maybe that is why the crystal diamond that represents the fire element is brown."

Gerwyn, who was sitting next to Joslin and eating his breakfast, stopped and patted his mother's arm. "That's great, Mom."

"It is sort of a puzzle," Joslin admitted. "The green diamond represents the earth element because it pertains to fertility, like the forces that work to keep the Indus Valley green. It goes in the eastern groove and symbolizes the springtime of the year."

"The clear diamond goes in the center and symbolizes the astral realm," Yuri added. "The yellow diamond fits in the northern portion of the grid and represents winter. It refers to the wind element, which is important in change and dreams."

"Let's go check out the brown diamond that apparently is located at the entrance to the Singing Cave," Joslin suggested. "I don't want to jump to any conclusions about the stone's significance until I have it in my hand. The Neanderthals must be the guardians for that rock."

Moments later, they stood outside the Singing Cave in Tibet. Yuri's father emerged from behind the brush and presented the stone to Joslin.

Joslin smiled and winked at her father-in-law as she took the stone. She was amused by his new role in the scheme of her universe. He smiled at her in return. Knowing that he was a man of few words, Joslin did not speak. Instead, she turned and headed toward the cave.

"Thanks, Dad," Yuri offered as he waved good-bye. "We can take it from here."

The Neanderthals surrounding them nodded and waved with appreciative smiles. The family returned the brown crystal diamond to the Four-Directions grid and stepped back to study the new, emerging patterns on the walls. Immediately, Joslin recognized the shapes and symbols.

"Oh my gosh!" she cried. "These are tarot card symbols concerning the four fixed signs of the zodiac. It is about our destiny and future in the wheel of fortune."

"Well, at least we are on the upswing," Yuri remarked, nodding his understanding of the symbol's significance. "Sometimes I wonder about our future."

Joslin cast him a sideways glance before planting a quick kiss on his cheek to reassure him. Then she resumed her focus on the planetarium.

"I know it's complicated," she admitted with a sigh. "Here, it is carved in stone, though these are only reflections from the fires within."

"Yeah, it's heavy." He shrugged with a wry grin. "I never would have guessed this pattern."

"Those are the zodiac signs for Aquarius the Angel, Taurus the Bull, Leo the Lion, and Scorpio the Scorpion," Elissa explained as she sauntered into the planetarium. "Don't think that you can get too far without your dragons!" she hollered at them.

"Oops!" Joslin replied with facetious emphasis as she lay back down on her bedroll and studied the constellations. She insisted, "We didn't go too far. Yuri's father handed us the brown crystal diamond just outside the entrance of the cave. We wanted to give you and Ivan some time alone. You've arrived at the right moment."

"Great, because it gets heavy," Elissa replied, feeling assured that she had been heard. "It's too late to say you're sorry."

"We've noticed," Yuri said.

"Why was Elissa yelling?" Gerwyn asked as he sat down next to his mother.

"She was beginning to feel left out," Joslin explained as Yuri flanked her on the other side of his son. "I think that she has a story to tell."

"You better believe that I have a story to tell," Elissa stated.

"Where's Ivan?" Yuri asked, slightly changing the subject.

"He wanted to go fishing," Elissa answered before continuing. "Getting back to the story…"

"Please continue," Joslin encouraged. She was willing to pay attention now.

Joslin snuggled closer to Yuri and distracted him from further interrupting thoughts. Yuri smiled contently and quietly. Joslin knew that Yuri would have difficulty sitting still through stories about his father.

Elissa nodded at Yuri before beginning. "A long time ago, the Neanderthals held most of the settlements in Eurasia. These celestials arrived from the Draco star system where the spirit of the earth was conceived. The passage was a huge success. Unfortunately, the Grays broke through the earth's defenses, and several lasers hit the planet. The lasers had the same effect as giant meteorites. Many Neanderthals died. As a result, they refused to participate in the Atlantean treaty. Although the Serpentines had never been able to penetrate the earth with their weaponry, the Neanderthals mistrusted them. They sensed that the Grays and Serpentine Federation were allies. The Atlantean Treaty excluded Serpentine derivatives such as the Grays, Blues, and Black Dogs."

Elissa paused for a moment. Everyone was listening attentively. The golden Sea Dragon queen glanced at the constellations above her on the cave walls. Gaining inspiration from the fixed zodiac signs on the corners of the wheel of fortune, she took a deep breath and continued. "The Serpentines put in a crystal system to protect the planet from meteorites. A few Lemurian insurgents remembered that the Earth's geomagnetic field was thick enough to withstand any impact. Realizing that the crystals were merely infused with mind control devices, they saw through the cover up. The Neanderthals had been observing the Grays' bases in the night sky. When the insurgents disabled the fake missile defense system, they directed a real meteorite toward the Grays' main base. It fell in the Mediterranean and sunk Atlantis.

"For years the Neanderthals have been custodians of the fire element after the Serpentines' plot was exposed. Prior to the sinking of Atlantis, the Serpentines provided the fire element. It was given to them when the Four Directions grid was created during the intergalactic wars of ancient Egypt. Due to their connection with Draco, the Neanderthals provided immunity from the Serpentine Federation. They represent the spiritual truth of the planet and are symbolized by the fixed signs of the zodiac elements."

"It's too late for the Serpentines to apologize," Yuri said when Elissa paused for his commentary. "That is why the planet has a promising future."

"Great," Joslin said with a slightly mischievous grin. "I'm not apologizing either for keeping the planet. I want a future. Does anyone else want a future?"

Elissa rolled her eyes slightly at Joslin's play on the subject.

"Let's discuss that further," Yuri suggested and kissed her lips.

Elissa noticed that Joslin had locked his lips. The golden Sea Dragon queen frantically realized that her students were getting out of hand. Gerwyn, however, remained oblivious to the subtle dynamics in the planetarium.

"Gerwyn," Elissa whispered. "Class is dismissed. Time to frolic. Let's go find Ivan and search for more dragon eggs. Your parents are still technically on their honeymoon. First things first."

"Goodie!" Gerwyn sang out, quickly running out of Singing Cave with Smoke behind him. "Smoke, you might have some more buddies coming. Let's go find them."

Before they rushed out of the cave's exit, Smoke rolled his eyes at his mother. "When is this guy going to get it?"

"There are a few things he hasn't quite figured out," Elissa chuckled. "I was counting on that."

Chapter Twenty-Four

The lively art of

Finding something or someone

To cherish

And still being able to

Sing about it

Tune Reference: *Cherish*

----The Association

THE NEXT DAY, Joslin awoke beside Yuri on the floor of the planetarium.

"Where's Gerwyn?" she whispered.

"I distinctly remember everyone leaving the cave on an expedition to find more Dragon eggs," Yuri softly replied as he rolled toward his wife and began kissing her.

"Oh," Joslin said, "when is he going to get it?"

"I don't know, but I am here to make the most of his innocence," Yuri announced with determined overtures.

Joslin hesitated, but Yuri persisted.

"Did you have any dreams last night?" he gently asked.

"Yeah, I dreamed that I gave birth to a daughter," she admitted, her voice tinged with worry. "One more powerful than me."

"Now there's a better future for you," he said, continuing to plant voluptuous kisses over her. "You'll benefit from it in other reincarnations. That is why we try to improve upon the next generation."

Joslin laughed quietly at his insistence.

"Do you have a problem with powerful women?" he quizzed her without interrupting his lovemaking.

Joslin giggled.

"You will have to educate your daughter on how to be careful with her strength," he told her as he moved closer.

Joslin accepted his sensuous embrace. Slowing him down, she began to lightly caress his shoulders above her.

"Elissa is a great teacher," Yuri said in an unrelenting manner.

"I think that we should go find that next diamond," Joslin casually told him, though she did not refuse him. Without encouraging him further, she remained suspended in the moment. "You know, the blue one. It's near the Narmada River where the Shiva Lingam is found."

"All the more reason to create balance here," Yuri said and kissed her.

"Aren't you a powerful force today!" she commented, allowing herself to be seduced by his passion.

"I'm inspired," he said confidently.

"Did Ivan put you up to this?" she questioned.

"Are you kidding? And disrupt Elissa's class? He knows better." Yuri proudly smiled. You're the one who made the first wisecrack…without any apology."

Joslin relaxed. "It's too late."

"Yes, it is too late," Yuri admitted. "Diamonds, like Sea Dragons, are a woman's best friend. Diamonds are forever."

"I've always considered you a diamond in the rough," Joslin acknowledged.

"That's because I am." Yuri grinned.

****

The next morning, Joslin awoke slowly. This time she nudged Yuri and told him, "Now I really do want to get that blue diamond. Time to go."

"At your service, my queen," he merrily replied as he immediately rose from their bed.

"I'll find Gerwyn while you get breakfast," Joslin said. "Meet me at the kitchen table ready for duty."

They both laughed before hurrying in opposite directions. After preparations were made, the family boarded their dragons and flew to the area along the Narmada River where the Shiva Lingam had been discovered. Kuan Yin stepped out of the jungle brush to greet them. She presented them with the brown crystal diamond.

"It's all in the family," Yuri acknowledged.

"And with a note of compassion," Kuan Yin added with a smile.

"Is that what last night was all about?" Joslin playfully nudged Yuri.

Yuri shrugged. Then he whispered discretely in Joslin's ear, "The divine universe moves in mysterious ways."

Joslin blushed. Wishing to get back to his dragon egg hunt, Gerwyn quickly seized the diamond from Kuan Yin's palm and handed it to his mother. The time traveling goddess softly laughed at Gerwyn's single-minded sense of purpose. Then she stepped back into the confines of the forest vegetation.

"We're in a hurry," he explained.

"I see," Kuan Yin answered, almost disappearing in a portal behind a large fern. "Your mom and dad can figure the rest out. No explanations needed. Back to your dragon egg hunt."

"Got it," Joslin announced as she tucked the diamond inside her cloak and waved Kuan Yin off.

Gerwyn reluctantly accompanied his parents back to the Four-Directions grid. Without hesitation, Joslin placed the blue crystal diamond in its western position. More new images covered the walls of the planetarium.

"The western diamond was the last one," Yuri observed.

"That's because the sun sets in the west on this planet," Joslin answered. "It apparently is significant."

"It's an ending," Yuri commented. "If the last crystal diamond concerned the future, this blue-crystal diamond references the past."

"You're right," Joslin pondered.

"Time for me to go," announced Gerwyn, who had been studying the images while listening to his parents. "I'm done."

"You're right," Joslin admitted with a sigh. "You've been very patient. Thanks for your help. Off to your dragon egg hunt. Your dad and I will take it from here. Keep Elissa and Ivan busy for us. I'm not ready for any more lessons either."

"One of the images is a setting sun," Yuri pointed out after Gerwyn had left the area. He gestured toward the far end of the cave wall. "Compassion concerns itself with setting limits."

Joslin sat down on the bedroll that was still unfurled on the floor of the cave. The revelation caused her to feel slightly dizzy with its weight. She wanted to savor its meaning in a more relaxed pose.

"I don't know," she uttered, shaking her head. "What limits? This is getting too esoteric. I am not sure about our interpretations."

"The Four-Directions grid is done. That's it," Yuri agreed. "You're right."

"It has nothing to do with us," Joslin lied.

"Nothing to do with you and me," Yuri repeated as he sat down across from her.

Joslin burst into tears without offering an apology. Yuri put his arm around her and held her. He remained silent. Joslin began to hold on to him intently for the first time.

"I'm not sure I know what compassion means anymore," she sobbed. "I need to get out of the cave. I feel like I am losing my humanity."

"Don't worry," Yuri consoled her. "We are all right here. Nobody is going anywhere."

"It has been very intense during the past weeks," she confessed.

"Yes, you are beginning to need me as much as I need you," Yuri commented.

"You're right," Joslin admitted, drying her eyes. "You broke through that wall of stars, dreams, dragons, and diamonds. I have something real to cherish."

"Perhaps that is what makes it real," Yuri replied.

Joslin paused and smiled at his words. "Like a diamond, I have been molded and shaped by forces and circumstances relating to the Four Directions: passion of fire, winds of thought and being, growth and promise of the earth, and, finally, water through the shedding of tears in resolution."

"What will they think of next?" Yuri asked rhetorically, and then he beamed at his wife. "The center of the Four-Directions grid is heaven itself."

"I must be pregnant," Joslin reasoned. "I feel like I am on an emotional seesaw."

"That's all right by me," Yuri said. "Seesaws are great tools for learning about balance."

"Is this a conspiracy?" Joslin asked in a forthright manner.

"Sort of," Yuri admitted. "I always wanted a daughter. Elissa thought that it would be great for Gerwyn to have a human playmate. She is becoming exhausted looking for dragon eggs with him."

"I'll play by the rules," Joslin decided as she looked up and saw Gerwyn returning to the planetarium. She gazed at him tenderly and motioned for him to sit down beside her.

"I think I am done looking for dragon eggs," he announced. "Maybe later. I'm hungry. How about if I prepare dinner for tonight? We could have a picnic outside of the cave. See some real stars for a while."

"Great idea, Gerwyn," Joslin answered. "We can camp together right under the stars."

She rose and extended her hand to Yuri, who was rising to his feet. Instead of grasping it, he kissed it. Then he rose on his own two legs.

"You have to know the rules to break them," he insisted.

"It never really ends," Joslin said, misty-eyed, as she took his arm.

"It only sets like the sun in a warm, golden light," he observed. "We'll see what you have to say about things tomorrow after a good night's rest."

"That's right. You've been keeping me up all night," Joslin teased lightly.

"You are very entertaining," Yuri mused.

"You two are beginning to finally sound like you are on your honeymoon," Elissa said as she walked toward them in the cave. "We had to get you to Singing Cave for it to happen."

Chapter Twenty-Five

The lively art of

Being able to strut

And romance to a beat

Has made for many great evenings

Tune Reference: *In The Evening*

----Led Zepplin

THEY RETURNED TO the honeymoon suite on Lake Hovsgol and remained there another week before they left for Utopia as previously scheduled. Joslin assumed her duties as queen and life continued relatively uneventfully. Nine months later, she delivered a healthy baby girl. They named her Twyanwedd, but called her Tinka, in honor of one of the Australian aborigines from the Southern Cross portal.

"You are going to need this," Kuan Yin said when she paid Joslin a surprise visit.

Joslin continued to nurse the newborn and did not get up. She was resting in bed with the baby. It had been a very busy day.

"Don't let me interrupt," the time traveling goddess insisted. She placed a twenty-centimeters-tall golden statue at the base of the bed. The figure reminded Joslin of Kuan Yin.

"Why, Kuan Yin, it looks like you," Joslin observed. "How wonderful! I'll look at it every time I need to remember that there is a goddess."

"I know but keep it as our secret," Kuan Yin told her. "It's called a golden tara, which refers to the tears of Buddha. They are really my tears. Somebody decided to deify them and give my ex-life partner the credit."

"Good job, Kuan Yin," Joslin replied. "I'll remember that. So far Yuri hasn't left me for the monastery, though Gerwyn is scheduled in a few years. He can't wait to join his cousins Illtud and Dewi."

"It's protective," Kuan Yin emphasized. "Buddha's blessing comes with it. I recently ran into him in another incarnation. He is busy helping the Aztecs with the Serpentine invasion. Tinka's birth and his work signify a new paradigm."

Joslin nodded and listened attentively as Tinka nursed peacefully.

"The birth of Gerwyn represented hope for many," the goddess began. After a short pause, she added, "Now by some off-chance, we have another birth. In the words of my friend, Avalokiteshvara, 'Sweet are the fruits of hope that is fulfilled. They who let go of hopes, however, live in peace. '"

"There you have it!" Joslin exclaimed in a hushed voice so that she didn't wake her semiconscious baby. "I have peace now! I've given up all hope."

"That's it. Thoughts are energy that can be used to create your own world," Kuan Yin replied. "Peace has got to start somewhere on the planet. It might as well begin with a busy career woman who is also the mother of two small children."

"Oh thanks," Joslin said. "I lost all hope on the tenth consecutive sleepless night. Yuri is still hopeful, but I feel like I've gone over the edge of the universe. Tinka is very demanding. I will always cherish this golden tara and the golden tears of compassion."

"Enjoy your peace," Kuan Yin answered. "I'll check in again later. Maybe they will make a golden replica of you nursing Tinka next. It will be in vogue. Call it 'my lady' in Italian so that even the Roman Serpentines will understand the message of peace."

"'My lady' in Italian is *madona*," Joslin said; she had almost nodded off into a peaceful sleep herself. Tinka dropped her latch on her mother's breast and dozed in Joslin's arms. Rearranging her position on the bed, Joslin told Kuan Yin, "'Madona with Infant' is a wonderful name for a work of art. I'm sure it will be popular, but first I'll sleep on it. For now I'll stick with the golden tara. Tinka seems content with being a Buddha baby."

The time traveling goddess left as quickly as she had entered. Joslin stared at the golden tara while the baby resumed nursing. The golden light reflected off the tara filled the room and inspired Joslin. For the first time since the wedding almost a year ago, she had a sense of where she wanted to go. There was something to be said for inner peace and the ability to draw on it for strength, especially in the times ahead.

****

When Tinka became six years old, she entered the convent in Wales. Her older brother, Gerwyn, had passed his Dragon flying tests the previous year and he went Alfie on many expeditions across the British Isles. They did so well that the populace began referring to Alfie as King Alfred the Great. Meanwhile, Gerwyn, followed his mother's tradition of orchestrating from behind the scenes. With so much intermarrying between the Roman

Serpentines, they prudently kept their identity a secret to the masses. Only those who could enter the portals knew the power behind the thrones.

From an early age, Tinka possessed enough strength to walk in both worlds. She could mingle with the locals and still remain connected to Utopia without blowing its cover. The common folk suspected that she had a connection with Utopia, but they began to simply call it the divine. Former traditions of the natives became obscure because of the need for secrecy and the deliberate attempt by their enemies to control their inner world. Sometimes it was simply a matter of updating the old practices to fit with the demands of the present. Those who did not have a grasp of the old practices became lost and easily manipulated by the jaded ways of the Serpentine rulers.

For the moment, the convents and monasteries served as safe havens for those who wanted to maintain a connection with the native spirit without having to fight for it. Originally intended as a way to exclude them personally, vows of chastity continued to intimidate the Serpentines. As long as they felt that they owned the convent and monasteries, they never meddled in them. Though attracted by the discipline and loss of identity, the sense of community in the convents and monasteries repelled the Grays. Most Grays had difficulty finding the light within and without, often dropping out as novices, wondering what the commotion was about.

Those who knew how to work the system found freedom. As designated virgins they could cultivate their former Druidic existence right under the protection of the Serpentines themselves. This occurred for hundreds of years until the Dark Ages, when all knowledge was lost, including the Serpentines'. This resulted an equal playing field, and everyone had to start from scratch or else learn to meditate. Others just learned how to exploit, which really wasn't anything new.

Tinka foresaw these upcoming events at an early age. Joslin rebuilt the past, whereas Tinka built for the future. Joslin sensed the importance of providing a firm foundation for Tinka and her work. She visited the convent in Wales so frequently via the portals that they began referring to her as Divine Mother. Those working toward the future in the midst of the present chaos viewed Joslin and Utopia as reminders of a glorious potential. As a result, they revered their connection through the portals.

"Divine Mother will appear at noon behind the sacristy," Tinka informed Dewi when he delivered some candles to the convent.

A tunnel that led from the sacristy to the nearby convent served as a private route for those wishing to visit the nuns. Dewi used it often to visit his girlfriend in the convent. By the age of sixteen, he had successfully passed his exercises as a Dragon flyer. His girlfriend, Dywnwen, was one of Tinka's closest friends.

"Great, let's make a party out of it. I'll tell Abban, Ailbe, Elfin, Justinian, and Glywys. We'll bring the bread. You can bring the wine. I think there is some leftover cheese from Dad and Cliges's party last night. They spent a long night talking things over with your mom. Something's up."

Tinka smiled at Dewi. "I know. Mom left the golden tara in the sacristy with Uncle Arthur. It's a sign that the next mission involves the Hill of Tara."

"Do you mean the ancient kingdom of the Tuatha dé Danaan?" Dewi asked.

"It's another history lesson," Tinka remarked. "I'll bring Gobnait, Tydfil, and Canna."

"What does the golden tara have to do with the Hill of Tara?" Dewi pondered out loud.

"In an earlier incarnation, Kuan Yin's older brother led a group from Atlantis to the Utopia region. Their mission was to establish a settlement before the Great Cataclysm. The golden tara is really a symbol of the Atlantean revolution. The tears of Buddha really began at the time of the Great Cataclysm. In a past life, Buddha had been an earth spirit that suffered as a result of the Serpentines' genetic warfare."

"I see the dharma between Kuan Yin and Siddhartha," Dewi commented softly. "Both suffered as result of direct Serpentine intervention in the life force of the planet. It was a marriage between the earth spirits and the Celestials that nurtured the planet."

"Through freeing themselves, they free us through their compassion," Tinka added.

"Now there's mastery for you," Dewi said with a whistle. "By overcoming suffering, an individual learns compassion. Compassion only happens when it is shared. It takes two."

"It is time to bring mercy to the Hill of Tara," Tinka murmured in a low voice.

Chapter Twenty-Six

The lively art of

Sidestepping one's ego

And maintaining balance

Tune Reference: *Take It Easy*

----Eagles

"WE GOTTA LIGHTEN up," Joslin said when she met with the group assembled in the sacristy. "Time to rebuild Avalon, only we'll give it a different name to create greater harmony with the locals. We need to continue educating our children. The word is out that the Serpentine authorities are building a new abbey in Glastonbury. We'll construct it for them, take over operations, and exist without being noticed. The new Avalon will be called the Glastonbury Abbey. We'll locate it near the Tor."

"Mother Superior mentioned the renewed Serpentine interest in Avalon," Conna said.

"Yes, she is aware of it," Joslin answered. "Though we are aware of the danger, ignorance can be even more dangerous. It is not a legacy that we wish for our children and their children. A cardinal by the name of Michael will be helping us with this project. We plan to make it the sister site for the one that already exists on the Hill of Tara. Patrick and the High King Lugaid have taken in the refugees from Scotland there. The Scots call King Lugaid

'Moluag.' It is his church name. The Serpentines who own the churches don't recognize him."

"We are beginning to outgrow the monastery here," Dewi commented after Joslin had paused for their reaction. "The Hill of Tara and Avalon have Ormuz towers, ones engineered by King Ormuz. The Tower of Tor still exists on Avalon. The remains of Joseph of Arimathea's palace lie in Glastonbury. The old Roman fort is also in disrepair. We can construct a new abbey at Glastonbury palace and place a fort around the Tor. This time the fort will protect Avalon rather than house Roman Serpentines."

"Dewi, that's a great idea," Tinka said. "The fort will help protect the nunnery and provide a screen from landing spaceships. What do you think, Mom?"

"Sounds good to me," Joslin said. "I can intercede with the locals, Utopia, the universe, and the Hill of Tara. The Serpentines and others are trying to land their spacecrafts on the planet again. They want to bring back the intergalactic wars."

"Is that why you wish to grid the Hill of Tara in the Four Directions?" Tinka asked.

"Yes, it has proven to be our best defense against the invaders," Joslin answered. "Meeting adjourned."

"What is Dad doing these days?" Tinka questioned curiously. She had many more questions but didn't want to overwhelm her mother further.

"He and his band of Dragon flyers are teaming with the Huns to take back their country and protect their Neanderthal ancestry," Joslin replied. "We plan to go on vacation when he returns from the latest Bulgarian invasion. Constantinople hasn't realized that the Slavs exist yet. Give them another hundred years and the Slavs will be making the Roman history books. By the time Constantinople falls, we'll have our own leaders. Until then, the Kazakhs, as some call Yuri's unique horde of Dragon flyers, prefer to be silent and carry a large club."

"So everyone is on the move," Ailbe summarized.

"We need to make a stand while we still can," Joslin said as she moved toward the feast waiting on a table at the other end of the room. "Let's have some bread and wine. Did anyone bring the cheese? The cheese that the monks on the Hill of Tara have been silently making is wonderful. As long as they keep making cheese, the Serpentine rulers don't ask questions about the abbey there. Vows of silence stop any inquiry by the Serpentines. Of course they talk to each other, just not to Serpentines. Great food is becoming one of our best tools."

The young monks began serving the feast while the young women poured the wine. Joslin thought a moment and munched on a piece of bread. Then she slowly began sipping her wine.

"I think that I am getting this transparency operation down," Tydfil remarked as she accepted her plate from a young monk. "Instead of fighting the current, I am riding with the tide to get where I want to go."

"That's it exactly," Joslin commented as she helped herself to some more bread. Then she added, "The young men have learned how to make great bread."

"It is not just an art, but it is a discipline." Abban grinned. "Our sisters love a man who can cook."

"It's a great skill to have in this present world." Joslin smiled. "After we are done here, Dewi and Tinka can help me grid the Hill of Tara in the Four Directions. It is about time that we cover this angle on affairs there. Those Atlantean refugees haven't gotten over the loss of their civilization.

Dadgon and Patrick have been busy keeping Ceredig out of the way. He is still looking for Non after all these years. It's odd how these Serpentines are always mourning the lost sheep instead of taking care of what they have. It leaves a wide hole for us to come in. Little does he know that Dadgon's son, King Lugaid, is running a Celtic kingdom right underneath his nose."

Dewi smiled. "Mom and Dad are very clever with disguises. Dad said that he'd help me with the Glastonbury project."

"Yes, I talked to Arthur last night," Joslin mentioned. "By the time our Saxon cousins arrive in Glastonbury, the abbey and fortress at Tor can hand the country right over to them. The Roman Serpentines consider themselves Britons now. A real Briton has Saxon relations, no Saxon enemies. Conscription and rape do not count as marriages in our history books. Constantinople ignores the Serpentine Romans here. They are convinced that everyone is fighting among themselves. At least, that is the story in Constantinople. It is merely a projection. Let's keep it up. Stupidity is their folly. Rather than educate their young, they consume them. Tomorrow let's go grid the Hill of Tara and show ourselves some mercy."

The next day, Dewi and Tinka accompanied Joslin to the Hill of Tara. Their transparent dragons flew high in the sky and hid them from view on the ground below. They left their dragons with some caretakers at the abbey and walked toward a translucent marble pillar that stood almost nine meters high. Together they arrived at the Stone of Destiny, or *Lia Fail*, a monument on the top of the hill. The Stone of Destiny, also known as Jacob's Pillar, was an Ormuz material used for a variety of purposes. One of its functions was to define leadership and determine rulers, often used in the coronation ceremonies of the high kings of Ireland.

"Looks like I'm still king of Wales," Dewi remarked as he touched the pillar and heard three soft hums. "Sometimes I spend so much time underneath this monk's hood that I forget my own true identity."

"That's why they made it for Jacob," Joslin commented. "It works for anyone, regardless of whether or not they are leaders. Jacob had so many wives, concubines, and children that he couldn't hear himself by the end of the day. He also had to deal with his half-brother, who had seized everything in typical Serpentine manner. It served as his touchstone, providing mental clarity. It also grounded his energy in a constructive manner. He'd wrestle with celestials all night to practice for daily affairs. By morning, he was charged and ready to go. However, he had to ground the energy so that he didn't electrocute himself and others. That would have been too forceful and unproductive."

"What is that red slab of sandstone next to it?" Dewi asked, pointing to a smaller piece of granite on the ground.

"Oh, it is a decoy," Joslin answered. "It looks impressive. Lugaid left it here for someone to steal. He wanted you both to have a good look at it first so that you'd be able to identify it later. This one screams instead of hums. It will sound an alarm all over the world."

"Got it," Tinka and Dewi replied in unison.

"Maybe we should give it to Fergie," Dewi added with a mischievous wink at Tinka.

Tinka laughed. "The Serpentines want him to come to Glastonbury and celebrate mass for them. They don't know that this priest is really Lugaid's son."

"There's an idea," Dewi murmured. "He can help me establish Glastonbury Abbey and then take the stone with him when he decides to become king of Scotland. He has already been placed there by the Stone of Destiny."

"All in due time," Joslin sighed, placing a restraining arm on Dewi's elbow. "That's what happens when they try to use our stuff for their purposes. The result is a mismatch made in heaven," Joslin said sarcastically. "I don't know why they do it. It just separates them further from the truth. Don't get me started."

"OK, Mom. We are doing this the transparent way," Tinka said. "Let's get gridding."

"Wait, there's more," Joslin said. "Before we start with the Four Directions, we must reconnect with the soul transport network, or STN."

"What?" Tinka and Dewi exclaimed in unison.

"Mom, you're getting spiritual on us," Tinka realized.

"Well, its something that Gerwyn has been working on with Fergus," Joslin admitted.

Chapter Twenty-Seven

Always have a plan

And go for the best

Tune Reference: *Spirit In The Sky*

----Norman Greenbaum

"FIRST, WE PLACE the golden tara on the altar in Tara Hall," Joslin instructed as she walked from the Destiny Stone to the great hall where the Celtic Dragon flyers assembled.

When they entered the great hall, they placed the golden tara on the small table. The Lia Fail was south of the tara. West of the Hill of Tara was an earth berm known as Rath Granne, the protected site where space platforms landed. Roman soldiers had once conquered the Hill of Tara. For almost five hundred years, they had occupied the region. Patrick had been successful in regaining it after one of the Grays' spacecrafts exploded on the site. Celtic warriors came pouring in from the portal in the Mound of Hostages and drove the Roman soldiers back to Rome. The portal was created during the time of the intergalactic wars in ancient Egypt.

"Take this cup of water that Lugaid left on this altar and pour it over the middle of Rath Granne," Joslin told Tinka and Dewi. "Then bury the cup there."

When they had finished, Dewi and Tinka met Joslin at the opposite end of Rath Granne. A single hawthorn tree stood in the east. A nest of doves could be seen in one of the higher branches.

"A fairy tree," Tinka said when they had reached Joslin.

Joslin reached for a dove feather that had fallen on a lower branch. She handed the feather to Dewi. Several White fairies fluttered overhead, hiding within the confines of the tree's foliage.

"Take this to Glastonbury, Dewi," Joslin said. "It is a message from the fairy kingdom. They agreed to help with communication between the two sites. The dove feather represents peace. In combination, the White fairies, doves, and hawthorn leaves represent the element of air. Air in this instance means communication."

"Got it," Dewi quickly replied, stashing the dove feather in a pocket of his monk's cloak.

"Wait, Mom," Tinka urged. "You're moving too fast. I'm not sure I understand what is happening here and what has taken place before us."

"The Mound of Hostages, Hill of Tara, and Tor are all connected," Joslin explained. "When the soul transport network collapsed during the intergalactic wars of ancient Egypt, we needed a new system." Joslin paused and then apologized. "I am still emotional about it. I'm sorry I breezed over some of the minor points. These three sites comprised the new system."

Joslin sat down on a log and rested for a moment. White fairies continued to lightly flutter in the sunbeams. Dewi and Tinka explored the forest around them. They remained in the vicinity before eventually sitting down next to Joslin.

"The final site for this Four-Directions grid is in the north. We can walk there together," Joslin decided. Then she explained, "The earth berm at

Rath Granne symbolizes hearth. The water was from the Nile River. It came through the Mound of Hostages portal. The Lia Fail represents prosperity."

"These are more mental themes rather than elemental," Tinka remarked.

"Yes, we are making a stand on these cerebral issues," Joslin replied. "We are getting more sophisticated in these complex times. It all started with the need for Jacob's Pillar, which represented the celestial link with the human family. Jacob was smart enough to decide that he needed one. The rest of the human family was off course and aligning with the Serpentine agenda. Speaking of which, the theme of the northern site is concerned with loss of innocence."

"Is that such a good thing?" Tinka pondered out loud.

"We will transmute the energy and elevate it," Joslin answered. "We must recognize the fact that we have all lost our childhoods. This realization frees us to move forward by correcting this casualty for future generations, which is one of the purposes of the abbeys and monasteries. We need a safe place to grow, learn, and heal."

The group began walking toward the earth berm. A breeze stirred through the brush surrounding the site, exposing a level area. Some of the rocks in the berm reflected the metamorphosis associated with intense heat. The transformation in the rocks was characteristic of a spaceship's landing pad.

"It's a burial site," Tinka observed when they had reached the northern position on the grid.

"It's a king's grave," Dewi commented.

"Yes, this is where you can commune with your grandfather," Joslin said.

"King Arcas?" Tinka asked with a puzzled expression on her face.

"Yes, the northern site is concerned with ancestry," Joslin said, gazing at the words inscribed on a tombstone. "It helps to know your roots."

"Wow! You mean they brought him all the way over here?" Dewi questioned.

"In a sense," Joslin replied. "The ashes from his funeral pyre were scattered here. It fits with the theme of air and communication."

"Right." Dewi sighed. For the first time in his life, he felt a connection to the past. It was in the air all around him. It soothed and comforted the heartache inside. He had never met his grandfather, who had died before his father was born.

After a moment's pause, they turned toward the center of the grid. Then they left to retrieve their dragons. Elissa was found munching on ferns in the underbrush. The transparent dragons twinkled in the sun's rays from the setting sun. They boarded their dragons, and Dewi flew straight to Glastonbury. After leaving Tinka at the sacristy, Joslin returned to Utopia.

Dewi arrived in Glastonbury and left Blue in the surrounding forest. Then he walked over to the church, where he met his father in the foyer. The king, who was wearing a monk's robe, appeared from behind several shelves of books.

"How's Joslin?" King Arthur asked his son.

"Just as fit as ever," Dewi replied, lowering his hood with a grin. He quickly surveyed the church as if sizing it up for a remodel. Then he showed the dove's feather to his father. "She said that this is for gridding the Glastonbury Abbey."

"Great job," his father commended. "There's one more thing that we'll need for the gridding."

"What's that, Dad?" Dewi quizzed.

"We'll need the Grail that Joseph of Arimathea threw in Chalice Well," Arthur replied.

"Do you mean the one that Perceval calls the Holy Grail?" Dewi questioned.

"Yes, we need to find it before he does. It is part of the Four-Directions gridding," Arthur answered.

"Perceval? What is he doing looking for the Grail?" Dewi asked. "I thought that he was still mourning the death of Pellinor, his father."

"He thinks that if he can retrieve the Grail, then it will make everything all right with the Serpentines," Arthur quipped. "He is addled like his father. There is no dealing with the devil. We could use that Grail and the healing waters from the well."

"We could bottle the water and distribute it through the churches," Dewi observed. "Call it holy water. It could be a way for those who seek refuge in the churches to throw off the Serpentines and Grays. I understand that it is protective."

"That's a great idea," Arthur agreed. "Anything that is healing is also protective against the Serpentines. Meet me at the Chalice Well. We need to go separately so that we are not detected."

A few minutes later, Dewi met his father at the Chalice Well. He noticed several translucent, White fairies fluttering over the well. A hawthorn tree rose next to the well. Other fairies of different colors remained twinkling in the confines of the branches.

"The dove feather summons the White fairies," Arthur revealed. "They are the strongest and have agreed to enter the well. You catch the Grail when they bring it up. I'll run interference by waving the white feather so that the

Serpentines are unable to remotely trace us. They would notice a sudden burst of divine grace on the planet if it were to resurface."

The operation went smoothly, and Dewi caught the Grail. Then he filled it with water from the well and stored it in a canteen to take back to Wales. He looked around at the beautiful gardens surrounding the well and Joseph of Arimathea's palace.

"The truth of the matter is that the Grail and well water represent all of our divine efforts concerning the light's revolution that graced the planet hundreds of years ago," Arthur said as he leaned over the well for a better look. Then he turned toward Dewi and reflected, "We are not alone. We have the support of the animals, plants, minerals, celestials, and MidEarth as well as our forebears. That's not a bad crowd."

"Can't be beat, Dad," Dewi agreed. "Let's do some elemental gridding."

"OK. The Chalice Well serves as the center point due to its connection with the divine and celestials," King Arthur began. "The new abbey will be the southern point. We'll bury the Grail underneath the cornerstone of the church."

Dewi smiled in approval. Then he interjected, "The Tor will be the western point. The fishpond will serve as the eastern point. People can reflect in the waters of the pond, whereas the well represents subsistence. The Tor symbolizes our decision to make a stand."

King Arthur nodded his consent before turning away and gazing wistfully into the distant north. He added, "The last point, the one in the north, may distress you. You must listen to me first so that you don't get upset. The northern point is one that Joslin and I discussed at the sacristy. The northern point is the site of the old Roman fort. All that is left are ashes.

We had many infiltrators there, and we are gridding them in commemoration."

Dewi's face whitened as he sighed. "That's exactly what we are doing now. The northern point is a reality check."

"Like the Lia Fail, it serves as a touchstone. It will keep the young initiates at Glastonbury Abbey from being too cocky and foolhardy," Arthur said. "It is the secret of our success."

"Point taken," Dewi said. "It's the thorn of the rose."

"And the hawthorn," Dewi's father concluded. "Bury the flower from the hawthorn at the northern point of the grid."

Chapter Twenty-Eight

Calling angels costs less

Than than calling 911

Tune Reference: *Calling All Angels*

----Train

SHORTLY AFTER GRIDDING Glastonbury in the Four Directions, Dewi hugged his father good-bye and returned to the Wales monastery on Blue, his transparent dragon.

"Joslin told us that we get to accompany you to Glastonbury to help with the new abbey," Gobnait mentioned when she met Dewi in the sacristy.

"Oh, it's so exciting!" Canna exclaimed. "We get to go by foot. For once we get to make our presence known. It's such a change from lurking in the shadows."

"It's a new dance," Dewi remarked dryly. "You know, it's called 'Lurking in the Shadows.'"

"Yeah, well, I'm ready for a new one," Canna said as she pointedly poked Dewi in the ribs through the thickness of his habit.

"Ouch!" he cried. "That hurts."

"Ha!" Canna answered. "You see what I mean. I am ready to kick the habit."

"Sounds good to me," he replied as he softened and moved closer to Canna. "I know what shadows lie underneath your habit."

Dewi was almost touching Canna with intimate familiarity when Gobnait interrupted the lovers. "Enough, you two. Later. Not in the sacristy. We need to stay focused. There's a reason why we are all hiding amongst the shadows. Don't blow it."

"You're right. Thanks," Dewi said, composing himself. "I almost forgot for one brief shining moment." Then he facetiously added, "We are saving our souls."

"Don't let it happen again, not until we are settled in the confines of the new abbey," Gobnait demanded. "Until then, keep to the convent under the watchful eye of Mother Superior. She wants us to pay a visit to the abbey at Pentre Ifan."

"Good thing she is on our side," Canna observed. "She is a fierce spiritual warrior."

"Great, we can visit Brynach on the way to Glastonbury!" he said happily. Dewi did a little dance in delight. Then he playfully commented with a slight shudder, "You are right, sister. We must keep ourselves pure and protected." Then he paused for a moment before adding with a wink, "I can't wait to start on that new abbey. We are going to make quite the holy family."

This time Gobnait poked Dewi in the ribs.

"Ouch!" he repeated in mock annoyance. "Oh, the divine punishments we must accept."

"Beat it, boy," Canna retorted as she turned toward the exit. "Meet us at the river at dawn. Bring your boat for the crossing of souls at Pentre Ifan."

"I'll try to be good, but its so hard," he whined jokingly as he folded his hands in prayer. "I beg for forgiveness."

"Forget it, you're not getting it," Canna teased. "There are dues to pay."

Both young women tossed their heads and laughed as they left the sacristy.

The next day, the threesome met at the river and loaded the boat with supplies. Then they headed upstream toward Glastonbury. Congregations from Wales lined the shore and waved.

"God bless," they called out to the two nuns and a monk floating down the river.

When they reached the dock, a monk came to greet them. He raised his hood and offered them his hand. "They warned me that I would have to fish you out of the River Nevern."

"Brother Brynach!" Dewi cried as he heartily hugged the hooded figure. Then he turned and helped the nuns out of the boat. "It isn't the same as the Nile, but it works much better these days for transformational purposes."

"Thank you, Brother Brynach," Gobnait said as she climbed out of the boat. "Where's Sister Cerridwen?"

"Oh, she has been busy mending wounded souls at Pentre Ifan," Brother Brynach replied in a more serious voice. "She went on vacation with her mother, the White fairy."

"Yes, I remember meeting her mother," Dewi recalled. Then he turned and explained to both nuns, "Our picnics were often chaperoned by our mothers. They guarded us during our field trips outside of the abbey."

After staying at the abbey near Pentre Ifan for a few days, they continued their journey to Glastonbury. Dewi steered the boat through various waterways until they reached their destiny in England. They docked at the water's edge and began hauling supplies to the Tor at the site once known as Avalon.

"Good thing the locals believe this place is haunted," Canna commented, surveying the wildflowers on the meadow. "I like the peace. I like the quiet. We obviously did a great job clearing it at Pentre Ifan."

"Let the Serpentine Roman Britons believe that it is still haunted," Canna commented as she peered over the meadow.

"So, when do the cute little monks arrive to help with laying the bricks?" Gobnait asked.

"Probably when you two get those bricks made," Dewi replied.

"Great, I'll get on it right away," Gobnait decided. "Bring them over. Tell them I am conducting classes on brick laying."

Dewi cocked his head to one side as he grinned at the double entendre. "I think that will entice them. There is something about brick lay-ying that brings a monk closer to the divine."

"My sentiments exactly. There's no time to waste," Gobnait said. "We have an abbey to build."

Dewi headed off immediately.

"Wait, you're leaving?" Canna called out as she raced after Dewi.

"You heard the woman," Dewi said as he turned and gently assured her. "I'll be back soon with help. You two need all you can get."

"You have a point." Canna smiled, drawing away slightly in reflection. Then she turned and headed toward the Tor. "OK, Gobnait, let's get on those bricks. We have got to have something to encourage those brick layers."

Work began immediately on the new abbey, and Dewi ceremoniously placed the Holy Grail underneath the cornerstone. After the abbey was three-quarters finished, they built a fort around it to further shield it from intruders.

Gerwyn came and joined them. He donned the monk's habit while Smoke puffed away to provide cover for the working crews. They wished for the extent of the construction to remain secret until they could fortify the abbey.

One late afternoon, King Arthur came to inspect the construction of the abbey.

"Good job, son," he told Dewi as he patted him on the back. "C'mon, Gerwyn, let's go pay a visit to Utopia and tell your mother about the progress."

They boarded their transparent dragons and trailed a slight distance behind the king's hot pink Sea Dragon. Alfred, the hot pink Sea Dragon, lit up the skies like a flaming sunset. People on the ground below turned their eyes to avoid being blinded by the light. When they reached the familiar Utopia, they dismounted and handed the dragons to caretakers. They rushed toward the dining area, where they found Joslin and Yuri entertaining guests from Bolivia.

"I'm glad you came," Queen Joslin said. "The delegation from Bolivia says that the Serpentines plan to attack Glastonbury Abbey."

"How do they know about affairs in England?" King Arthur quizzed.

"Pepe captured a Serpentine base in South America. They found a map of Glastonbury Abbey," Joslin said. "Now, who do you know that would give a map of Glastonbury Abbey to the Serpentines?"

"Obviously, we've been betrayed," Dewi remarked.

"Uh-oh!" Gerwyn almost shouted. "Nimue's half-brother did it. He left the order recently over a love affair that went badly. He became jealous when my lover rejected him."

Dewi looked at Gerwyn and agreed. "You're right. He became rude and didn't take no for an answer. He'll bring King Mark back to Cornwall. We had better hurry back. The entire nunnery may be threatened."

"Wait," Joslin said. "It could be a trap."

"You may be right," Arthur said, restraining his son and nephew. "I have a plan, but it is daring and ruthless."

"Let's have it, Dad," Dewi said, "before it is too late."

They stayed late into the night. When they were satisfied with their strategy, Gerwyn and Arthur returned to the Glastonbury Abbey on their dragons. Unfortunately, they were too late. The Serpentines had already pillaged the convent. Grief stricken, Gerwyn raced across the meadow to find survivors. Arthur called to him, but Gerwyn never heard him. An army of Serpentine Britons ambushed the monk at the riverbank. They tied him up and carried him off to prison. Meanwhile, Serpentine Dragons took turns puffing to illuminate the transparent dragon, and attacked Smoke.

Arthur and Alfred slaughtered the three Serpentine Dragons to free Smoke, who appeared severely injured. Then they rescued the surviving priests left hanging on the crosses. They freed those who were still alive from the crucifixions and attended to their wounds. Then they buried the dead so that their true identities would not be discovered, finding no surviving nuns or monks.

Joslin arrived with Dewi the next morning. The communications network at the abbey had been sabotaged. They were shocked to hear the news of the destruction and Gerwyn's capture by the Serpentine Roman Britons.

The next morning, they crept into the town of Glastonbury and watched the soldiers lead Gerwyn to the town square. He had been tortured throughout the night. Now the town authorities planned to publicly crucify him for retaliation. Joslin wept when she saw her son. Sticking to the original plan, she sent a flaming torch into the sky overhead. An army of Serpentine Dragons appeared, having instinctively responded to the signal. Their flyers on the ground below tried to wave them out of view, but it proved too late. Ignorant town people unfamiliar with the dragons screamed in terror at the ugly beasts flying above them. They fled the region, leaving behind only the Serpentine Roman Britons.

Yuri and his band of Siberian Dragon flyers appeared out of the cloud cover and attacked the confused Serpentine Dragons. Meanwhile, troops of elves from the MidEarth surfaced from a portal in the nearby woods and slew the Serpentine Roman Britons. Joslin rushed the town square and instructed Elissa to saw through the cross near Gerwyn's legs. The soldiers had already maimed him by nailing down his feet. Joslin cut the restraining cords on his extended arms. Arthur drew his sword and attacked the Serpentine guards around them. Taking care to avoid injuring Gerwyn's feet any further, Dewi lifted Gerwyn and the severed plank of wood onto the back of Elissa. Then he helped position Joslin next to Gerwyn before he joined his father in battle. Elissa flew immediately to Glastonbury Abbey.

"I want grandchildren," she whispered to him while Elissa landed on the meadow.

"Sorry, Mom." He smiled slightly before he winced in pain.

Several caretakers hurried toward the mother and son. They removed Gerwyn and lowered his body to the ground. He fell unconscious as the caretakers unpinned his feet from the wooden plank. Joslin cradled her son in her arms as the tears of a lifetime full of pain fell over him.

Chapter Twenty-Nine

Harbor love

For those who

Haven't lost their vision

Tune Reference: *Daniel*

----Elton John

FOUR YEARS LATER, prosperity returned to Glastonbury Abbey. Gerwyn recovered the use of his limbs and healed while his younger sister, Tinka, fell in love and married in a large, private ceremony at the Hill of Tara. Only the MidEarth and immediate family attended. They had won the battle at Glastonbury, and it would only be a matter of time before the abbot of Glastonbury officially turned the area over to the Saxons.

Tinka married Caradog, the grandson of a Merwyn named Bran the Blessed. After the Serpentines killed Bran with the other Merwyns, Caradog's father led an attack on Rome after defeating the Franks and seizing command of the Gauls. His father's name was Brennius. Though the victory had been short-lived, the ruse fatally wounded the city of Rome. Caradog, Brennius' son, remained at the Hill of Tara where his mother, a Danaan, raised him. The Danaans descended from the ancient kingdom of Tuatha dé Danaan, or Tribe of Dan, one of the twelve tribes of Israel. Only one woman remained of the Tribe of David, and she had immigrated to

Ireland with Dan's tribe. They intermarried with the Celtics and formed the Tuatha dé Danaan.

Shortly before the collapse of Atlantis, several groups of refugees fled to northern Asia. The Scythians descended from the Atlanteans, who had settled in northern Europe. They lived in dirigibles that floated in the air above the Earth's atmosphere to avoid the calamity below. They called themselves Santas, which meant divine. Most of them had endured heavy experimentation by the Serpentines and chose the name as a reminder to cultivate an inner sense of purity. The Arctos, on the other hand, aligned themselves with the new orientation of the Earth's polarity. They wished to keep their feet on the ground and observe the North Pole in the Bear constellation from afar. On Earth, they formed a unique relationship with the mighty white bear that inhabited the Arctic region.

The Serpentines pursued all Atlantean refugees on the planet. The surviving Santas established a new community in the surrounding mountains and later became known as Scythians.

During the intergalactic wars of ancient Egypt, a Celestial named King Nebuchadazzar restored Babylon after the Tower of Babylon had been destroyed by the Serpentines. Then he threatened to retake Jerusalem after the Serpentines infiltrated King Solomon's Temple. The majority of the ancient Hebrews, or human beings, had followed the path of Lilith and aligned themselves with the Serpentines. He sent an emissary to warn the remaining ancient Hebrews led by King Zedekiah. Unfortunately, the corrupt Hebrews killed the messenger. This broke the agreement established between the celestials and the human beings on the planet. A second messenger, Jeremiah, descended from Jacob through the fifth Tribe of Dan. He warned the ancient Hebrews and then attempted to secure the Ark of the Convenant as well as the Stone of Destiny.

One of the king's daughters, who had been observing Jeremiah, resisted her father and tried leaving Jerusalem. Called Teia Tephi, they imprisoned her along with Jeremiah. While King Nebuchadazzar purged the tribes of Israel of the Serpentine infiltrators, Jeremiah and the princess hid in a cave underneath the temple during the destruction. Afterward, they were freed and supervised the handling of the Hebrew artifacts. King Nebuchadazzar took Jeremiah, Teia Tephi, and the artifacts with him to Egypt, where they put the group on a spaceship of Scythians bound for Ireland. The Scythian mission was to confront the largest base of Serpentines.

A Scythian king, Nemed, attacked the enormous collection of Serpentines who had gathered in Ireland after fleeing Atlantis. The Scythians fought with a vengeance and defeated the Serpentines. They re-established the human family on the planet from the Houses of Dan and David. The descendants of Jeremiah, representing the House of Dan, were called Danaans. They named the site Hill of Tara, or Hill of Torah. When the Serpentines counterattacked several hundred years later, the Danaans took temporary refuge in the MidEarth. They hid the Ark of the Covenant there with Lia Fail and Four Magical Treasures.

Jeremiah had a Scythian wife, and Teia married one of their sons who had helped with the passage to safety. Named Dagda, he replaced King Nueda when he lost his arm leading the second invasion on the Serpentines. Nueda had succeeded Nemed after the Serpentines killed him by poisoning the water supply. This occurred shortly before the exodus to the MidEarth. Nueda had an invincible sword that had been given to him by the

Thunder People. Meanwhile, Jeremiah eventually realized that he could summon celestial spaceships by simply removing the lid on the Ark of the Covenant. Benevolent spaceships responded and presented Dagda with a Cauldron of Plenty, which he used to fortify his troops after the Serpentines contaminated their supplies. The Serpentines fled, and the Danaans won the battle decisively.

Tinka married Caradog in a hidden valley below the Hill of Tara. People entered the valley through a portal connected to the MidEarth. The couple walked through the magical, lush valley as fairies wove garlands of flowers around their heads. Birds sang and the Little People came out to dance around them. The air was fresh, light, and festive. Colorful flowers bloomed everywhere, and sparkling brooks glistened in the rays of sunlight blessing the valley. Puffballs of iridescent pollen floated through the air. Light Beings as small as a diatom rode the feathery balls. Far removed from the world around it, the hidden valley remained tranquil and idyllic.

When they reached the altar of Four Magical Treasures, the couple kissed. A leprechaun approached the altar with a present for Caradog's bride. It was a necklace with a stone from Lia Fail, one of the Four Magical Treasures. Caradog also wore one around his neck, though his was a little smaller and less powerful. He laughed merrily when he saw the size of the stone for his bride.

He smiled as he placed it around her neck and then whispered, "You need a bigger rock than me as high queen of Ireland."

Tinka softly laughed and assured him with a kiss. "Fal, who made the Lia Fail from which these stones are fashioned, wrestled with Jacob in the night. He called her an angel. The ancient Egyptians named her Shai, or fate.

We all must wrestle with our destinies, though they may not always be obvious at first.”

“You are wise, my love. Will you marry me?” Caradog replied, spontaneously rolling into the traditional words of the ceremony without pausing.

“I will,” Tinka responded, remaining quick on the uptake and matching his wit. Then she added, “Will you, Caradog, marry me as we follow our destinies together?”

“I will,” he answered before he whispered in a voice that only she could hear, “And miss out on all the action?”

Imaile, the celestial who presided over the ceremony, never had time to say, “You may now kiss the bride.” The couple had already embarked on a kissing spree. Instead of waiting for the ceremony to end, Caradog, valiantly swung Tinka into his arms and carried her through the valley. The hauflins, elves, leprechauns, fairies, celestials, and families cheered.

While others chased the bride and groom on to their honeymoon in Egypt, a small group gathered around Imaile and listened to his closing remarks. “The Stone of Fal glows whenever the wearer is around the magic of the divine,” Imaile explained. “It is especially for those who must live in the modern chaos of these times. It helps a human remember to keep looking for the fairies, the Little People, the celestials, the Light Beings…”

“The Lia Fail is one of the Four Magical Treasures. What are the names of the others?” Yuri, the father of the bride, asked.

“Dagda’s Caldron is one,” Imaile answered. “Caradog’s forebear was skilled in the arts and created a cauldron that would satisfy anyone’s appetite. It helps to keep peace if everyone leaves the Hill of Tara contented and fed.”

"Great idea." Joslin nodded to Yuri. "Maybe we should think about getting one for Utopia?"

"They dipped Gerwyn in it," Yuri said. "It is also known as the Cauldron of Rebirth. We all are born from the waters of plenty. It has been used to resurrect armies of slain warriors."

"I'm surprised that they didn't use it on Jesse, the Merwyn that they killed in the Hebrew uprising," Joslin said.

"Jesse had his own thing going," Imaile remarked.

Yuri shrugged a question at his wife. He didn't understand, but neither did she.

"The Spear of Lugaid is another one of the Four Magical Treasures," Imaile continued. "They forged with the fire of the Thunder People and gifted to Lugaid. It always finds its mark and returns to the one who threw it."

"Nice!" Yuri nodded, thinking of all the times that he could have used such a spear.

"The Spear of Lugaid must be used wisely," Imaile cautioned. "It is stored in a vat of water so that it doesn't burn the earth. It gets hotter with every mark it makes."

"Hotter and hotter," Joslin remarked. "There's the science of applied knowledge or appropriate use of technology for you. It was one of Atlantis' downfalls. It's called Wisdom."

"It is a wise spear," Imaile commented. Realizing that he was preaching to a tough audience, Imaile shrugged slightly with an air of resignation before going on, "The fourth object is the Sword of Light of Nuada. Like all the magical treasures, it is a spiritual symbol. The sword is invincible and cuts to expose the truth. It is double-edged and requires a balanced approach."

"I think that we handle that." Joslin nodded her head confidently as she cast a sideways glance at Yuri.

"Me too," Yuri agreed. "Yes, it truly was a marriage made in heaven."

Chapter Thirty

Tall orders

Define values

Tune Reference: *Get Together*

----The Youngbloods

Four years later, Gerwyn married Fergie in a simple ceremony at the Tor. The Glastonbury community and dignitaries gathered at the site that had once been known as Avalon. The men held each other in a firm handshake as Imaile officiated.

"Do you Gerwyn take this beautiful animus and future king of Scotland to be your life partner?" Imaile asked.

"I do." Gerwyn warmly smiled.

"Do you, Fergus, king of Scotland and priest of Glastonbury, take this fierce Glastonbury monk and king of the Reindeer People in Scandinavia, to be your life partner?" Imaile asked.

"I do," Fergie beamed.

"They are so handsome together," Tinka whispered to Joslin.

"Gerwyn loves everyone." Joslin sighed. "They will have no problem finding women who will want to intercede."

"It's the men that we worry about," Tinka whispered as the two women walked away from the gathering to continue their private discussion. "They get jealous. We can never be sure whether it is over the men or the women. Times are complicated."

Others in the congregation let them be. Imaile continued with his closing remarks while the mother and daughter freely embarked on their own commentaries. Gerwyn watched them drift away and grinned. Yuri and Caradog held hands and proudly acknowledged the blessed peaceful union.

"May you continue to cherish, heal, and bind each other's wounds like holy brothers," Imaile stated in a deep, gruff, masculine voice.

The women paused and perked their ears at Imaile's words. Joslin wiped a tear that had fallen from her eye. Tinka put her arm around her mother's shoulder and hugged her tenderly.

"After the love fiasco, Gerwyn swore off women," Tinka said, trying to comfort her mother. "He and Fergie had been working on the soul transport network and realized that they were soulmates. Like Noah's Ark, we must go two by two, at least."

Joslin nodded, drying her tears. "Fergie has been so wonderful for Gerwyn. He accompanied him to Scandinavia for recovery and protected him. He stayed with him throughout, dressing his wounds every night, attending to his needs, and even dipped him in Dagda's Cauldron that he borrowed for a night. I couldn't ask for a better son-in-law or ally."

"I know," Tinka sighed. "He's cute too."

"There is something about free love that makes even the gods and goddess jealous," Joslin observed. "Even Eros is just another god. I prefer the Druid policy of KISS: Keep It Simple."

"I know, Mom. The Druid ways are underground now, but they still exist in a free heart," Tinka assured her.

Joslin sobbed softly and nodded. The women embraced and held each other warmly.

After a moment, Joslin lifted her head from Tinka's shoulder. "It's our best offense, a free and wild heart."

Tinka raised her head and chuckled softly. "Some would even call it a sin, but it is how we are saving our souls. One soul alone is vulnerable to Serpentine interference. We learned that early during the intergalactic wars of ancient Egypt when they disrupted the Nile crossing."

"I see that you have been educated well," Joslin remarked and laughed. "Now about those grandchildren…"

"You have a few already," Tinka commented as she watched her small boy pounce on Gerwyn as the ceremony ended. "I learned that Gerwyn's lover was pregnant at the time of the Serpentine attack. She escaped when the Serpentines dropped her to pursue Gerwyn."

A weight fell from Joslin's shoulders. "I had a feeling that there was one more child."

She put her arm around Tinka and directed her farther away from the procession. Joslin wanted to be sure that no one could overhear them, especially Gerwyn. They stood in the shadow of the abbey walls.

"Nobody has the heart to go searching for the surviving nun. People are respecting her privacy given the circumstances. It took Gerwyn several years before he was strong enough to even stand. He had to live first. As everyone heals, I am sure the affair will come to light," Tinka said.

"Does Fergie know?" Joslin questioned.

"He is part Druid. He understands and suspects. Apparently the couple could send off sparks without even touching. It aroused the interest of the entire abbey," Tinka replied. "Fergie feels lucky to be connected to Gerwyn.

They make great allies. Also, the partnership diverts attention from Gerwyn's lover in hiding."

"Another marriage made in heaven," Joslin sighed as she resolutely ushered Tinka out of the shadows. "Let's join the crowd. We have a lot to celebrate. This establishes the soul transport network between three areas: the Tor, Hill of Tara, and Mound of the Hostages. The Mound of Hostages is where the high kings and queens are buried, much like the pharaohs of ancient Egypt.

"The Nile crossing broke for several reasons. It lacked balance, such as yin and yang. Also, most of the pharaohs proved to be too Serpentine in nature. They sunk the souls of their constituents, who tried to reconnect with the celestial realm during their transformation. Instead the white lights of the Serpentines' spaceships picked up the souls, where they remained, tortured and trapped in a vortex. The dolmen at the Pentre Ifan has been recovering the fragmented, wounded souls so that they can fully incarnate in the next life."

Tinka softly wiped away a tear that had escaped her eye. She hugged her mother firmly and then rejoined her family in the crowd. Yuri caught up with Joslin and took her arm in his. Together, they entered the dining hall and sat at the end of the table. The rest of the crowd took its time arriving for the feast.

A mist rose from the depths of the former Isle of Avalon, surrounding the Tor and hiding the inhabitants from view. The transparent dragons were visible in the mist, and everyone marveled at their exquisite beauty and strength. It was a rare sight to see so many Dragons in one space.

"Oh, what a strong, handsome couple!" Ivan told Elissa proudly. "Remember when Gerwyn was just a little man? Now he is old enough to get in trouble."

"We'll be flying to Scotland next," Elissa replied. "They will be establishing themselves there."

"Right on top of the fake Stone of Destiny," Ivan observed. "I hear that Fergie decided to bring it with him to the Scottish throne."

"Nobody else was using it," Blue added. "They tried to give it away, but even Ceredig's heirs aren't greedy enough for a wailing stone. Fergie wants to put it in place as a joke gift in case the Turks return."

"Maybe they should take it to Constantinople," Elissa suggested. "I understand that the throne there likes to play musical chairs."

"Hmm," Ivan began. "It would stop the show."

"Maybe we should mention it to Joslin," Elissa chuckled.

"Let's go, my dear," Ivan told Elissa as he offered his arm to escort her.

Joslin roared with delight when she heard of the strategy. "That's a great idea. It's too good of a joke for Constantinople. We can use a good laugh here." The Sea Dragons puzzled over Joslin's scheme. "Let's give it to the turncoat who betrayed the abbey to the Serpentines," Joslin explained. "The Serpentines put him on the throne as King Mark of Cornwall."

"Now I know where not to vacation," Ivan interjected.

Elissa poked her mate in the ribs.

"We are letting my Saxon cousins take care of the area," Joslin said decisively. "Fergie is placing the phony Stone of Destiny in the Scone monastery. Any disenfranchised heirs to the Serpentine throne will seek refuge in Scotland and use the Stone of Scone to prove his or her claim to any available throne. Gotta keep thinking about those grandchildren and their grandchildren."

"The rest of us will know better," Elissa concluded. "This way we will know who not to invite to the party."

"Cheers!" Joslin exclaimed as she and the Sea Dragons raised their chalices in a toast.

Chapter Thirty-One

Freedom,

A little known

Tall order

Tune Reference: *Born Free*

----Andy Williams

SHORTLY AFTER GERWYN and Fergie married, Dewi visited his childhood home of Pembrookshire near Pentre Ifan. He went there to visit his old friend, Brother Brynach, who was managing the monastery. Knowing that his friend was probably relaxing in his private quarters away from the abbey, he knocked on the wooden door of his friend's cottage unannounced.

"Hi, Dewi, great to see you again," Brynach answered. "You have a wonderful sense of timing. Do you remember our friend Cerridwen? She is here to help construct the new convent in the abbey."

Dewi entered the dimly lit cottage and allowed his eyes to adjust to the light. Slowly, he spied his old friend, Cerridwen. He had not seen her since leaving for Glastonbury almost ten years ago. She was been two years younger than him, and although he knew that she had grown, he was surprised by her appearance. Cerridwen had matured into a beautiful young woman. Now he stood awestruck in her presence.

Brynach watched the expression on his friends' faces and grinned. "Funny, I knew that you two would hit it off. Let's go to Lake Bala for a picnic. It will be just like old times."

The hooded woman and two monks boarded their transparent Dragons. Cerridwen flew on the back of Pinkie, while Brynach soared high on the wings of Goldenrod. Dewi rode between them on Blue. Within a short amount of time, they landed near the lake named for its beauty, Lake Bala. They left their transparent dragons on the shore and tore off their clothes. Then they raced each other for the lake and dove in.

They played underwater tag and took turns being the seeker. Finally, on one of Dewi's turns, he surfaced close to Cerridwen and kissed her.

"You're it!" he gasped, bobbing up and down in the water. Then he added with a twinkle in his eye, "When we are done playing, you will be known as the Enchantress of Lake Bala."

"Do you mean that you would leave me with nothing more than a reputation?" she asked rhetorically before diving under the surface to find better footing.

"How about an abbey?" he asked breathlessly while he watched her swim away.

"There's a start," she answered as she reached shallow water. Then she turned around and asked, "How about your first born?"

"We could give that a try," Dewi offered, swimming toward her.

"Our friend is leaving us," Cerridwen observed.

"He's a very good friend," Dewi admitted.

"Sorry, guys, I hate to set you up and run, but I must get back to teach some novices how to bake bread," Brynach announced as he dried his naked body and dressed hurriedly.

Out of the corner of their eyes, the couple watched Brynach leave on Goldenrod as they embraced each other passionately in the shallow water.

"It was not only Brynach who brought us together," Cerridwen whispered while she continued to seek firmer footing in the water. This time she turned toward a secluded spot on the shore. Taking his hand in hers, she said, "I knew it when I bonded with Pinkie."

"He always complemented Blue in a mystical way," Dewi agreed as he pulled Cerridwen toward him.

She stopped walking and succumbed to his pressure. He plunged inside her while lying in ankle-deep waves. Still swimming in her head, she found him deep inside her in a vague form within the white mists.

"Somehow we grew into our transparent dragons," she told him as they rode the clouds in a divine rhythm.

"No," he insisted between nebulous waves of consciousness, "it was your mother."

"What?" she gasped. "She's a White fairy."

"She was one of the White fairies that helped us retrieve Jesse's cup," he revealed. "It is underneath the cornerstone of the church at the Tor."

"I see that you are on a spiritual mission," she observed.

"Aren't we all?" he questioned.

"We will both be changed from this experience," she confessed. "We are divine shape shifters, intent on changing our destinies for the better."

"I love you," he told her breathlessly, "for soothing my soul and helping me find heaven on earth."

"It will always be here," she promised, "like a cauldron ready in a hearth fire."

"You will always be my inspiration for the divine," he acknowledged.

"Be my poet," she instructed.

"Always and forever," he promised.

For a brief interlude, they rested on the dry shore.

"I don't want to go back to the abbey," she told him in a daze.

"Don't," he instructed. "Stay here. Be free and enjoy the beauty of the lake."

"You'll have others," she acknowledged.

"Yes, so will you," he said in a hushed voice.

"I know." She sighed, almost regrettably.

"But this moment in time belongs to us," he concluded.

"Always and forever," she agreed before she lapsed into a deep sleep.

After she awoke, he dressed and bade her good-bye.

She wrapped a cloak loosely around her naked body and followed him to a small clearing in the woods. The transparent dragons puffed, filling the air with a light haze that concealed the lovers. Cerridwen watched the colored figures of the transparent dragons appear in the mist. Pink and blue lights swirled off the reflection of their scales. She gazed at the magical beauty of the sight as Dewi gave her a parting kiss. Then he smiled and looked around at the nearby woods.

"The giant that roams these parts will protect you," Dewi told her before he boarded Blue. "He loves you."

"I know," Cerridwen replied. Then she smiled. "We've met before."

"I know." He nodded and then winked at her. "Take good care of my daughter."

"I will," she assured him. "I had the same dream. Like the lake, she will be very beautiful."

"The new convent that Brynach is building will need a mother superior," he said with a sparkle in his eye.

"I will prepare her," Cerridwen asserted.

Then he left, circling once in the sky above before he disappeared.

Cerridwen finished dressing and began gathering stones for her new lakeside cottage. A few days later, the giant arrived to help her. His name was Teleg Foel.

"I heard that you were coming." She smiled.

"I heard that you needed help," he admitted. "You are pregnant with the next queen of Wales. That is very inspiring."

"We are rebirthing ourselves in freedom," she confessed.

"I know." He smiled. "Our King Dewi of Wales spends much of his life evading captivity. His mother, Non, barely escaped capture. He must be a very proud father."

"I know," she answered with a sparkle in her eye.

****

Seven months later, Dewi knocked at the door of her cottage. She met him at the entrance, personally opening the door for him. He admired her round, pregnant belly that contained his child.

Sweeping her in his arms, he held her as he whispered in her ear, "I have known you as a maiden. I have you as a lover, and I love looking forward to your wisdom as you further mature."

"Does that mean that I am a triple goddess in your eyes?" she questioned him, and a chuckle bubbled up from her nearly full womb.

"Yes," he almost cried. "I have already seen much death in my lifetime. Every time I see you I feel that my life has meaning."

"You are a poet," she told him as he nuzzled her with voluptuous kisses.

"Call me your bard," he insisted. "I am known by many names."

She turned toward him. "You are freeing us from the shackles of the Serpentines in England. It has been prophesied."

"I am happy to fulfill it," he answered as he took her in his arms again. "You are freeing me."

They made love in the bed near the hearth. He stayed for several days before leaving again for Glastonbury. Teleg supplied them with enough firewood for a fortnight.

"We have two children," he acknowledged. "One is our beautiful daughter, whereas one is an ugly dark son who serves as a knight for his father, King Arthur of England, through the graces of wit."

"I will prepare you for battle," she offered, casting an assortment of herbs into the cauldron over the hearth. "Looks may bring you a daughter, but ugliness will keep you alive in battle. Wisdom will serve you better in warfare."

"Oh, thank you, my love," he said, desperately clasping her hands in his for a single precious moment. Then he released her. "You consume me, transforming the deaths of my life into light."

"We must pay a visit to the portal dolmen at Pentre Ifan," she said as she kissed him. "Death is not an evil darkness, it is merely a transformation. We are all conceived in darkness and must pass from the womb to be born."

After breakfast they journeyed to the portal dolmen at Pentre Ifan. Cerridwen held his hand as they entered the portal. They walked in the darkness together.

"Wave your white dove feather," she instructed. "It summons the white Fairies," she reminded him. "White fairies retrieve soul fragments without breaking into fragments themselves. They have earned their strength. That is why they could bring up the Holy Grail from Chalice Well. The Merwyn's soul had fragmented under the duress. Some call it a miracle, but only love can produce true miracles. It was trauma, not love, that leaked the spirit of the Merwyn into the Grail. Love transformed it. Now we have a miracle called ourselves."

Several White fairies appeared in the darkness. One of them was Cerridwen's mother. She whizzed around Dewi's ears.

"You are a man of peace. You came in love," Cerridwen's mother acknowledged him. "Sometimes it takes darkness to be able to see the light."

Then the entire portal flooded with light and they entered the MidEarth. Dewi recognized the souls of those who had died in the attack on Glastonbury. A gentle tear fell down his cheek.

"Remember us," they told him. "We are with you. You are coming home to victory."

Chapter Thirty-Two

Don't be shy

When it comes

To what you need

Tune Reference: *Truly Madly Deeply*

----Savage Garden

WITHIN A YEAR after the picnic at Lake Bala, Cerridwen gave birth to a beautiful baby girl. She called the child Creirwy. Dewi was present for the birth and stayed for several months before he resumed duties elsewhere. He left her under the protective care of the giant Teleg Foel.

Four months after he left for Glastonbury, there was a knock on Cerridwen's door. Cerridwen answered the door with Creirwy in her arms. A nun greeted her with a basket of fruit.

"Grandchildren. I want to see my grandbaby," Non announced as she strolled through the open door.

"She is not very amusing yet, but she is very beautiful," Cerridwen said, handing the child over to Dewi's mother. Although she had never met the woman before that day, the family resemblance proved striking. "Here, I could use a break."

"Oh, she is so cute!" the proud grandmother exclaimed. "She has Arthur's blue eyes."

"Yes, there is no mistake in saying that she is the king's granddaughter," Cerridwen said, relaxing in a soft chair by the fire.

"That might come in handy," Non cooed to the baby. "Then again, it might get you in trouble one day, depending on how things are going."

"That's why we have nunneries," Cerridwen quipped. "So far Teleg and I have been doing just fine. Having a giant around keeps intruders away. At any rate, the girl will have career options between the lake and the abbey."

"Such a wonderful child," Non doted over the baby. "It is like falling in love again. I'm so glad you seduced Dewi. He wasn't quite the same after the attack on Glastonbury."

"I wish that I had seduced him," Cerridwen admitted. "What a dove feather in my cap would that have been! No, all Dewi needed to do was go jump in the lake."

"I'll have to tell him to go jump in the lake more often," Non agreed. "You gave him a whole new career. When he is not fighting the Serpentines or running abbeys, he wanders through towns as a bard called Taliesin."

"It is great to be able to write your own history," Cerridwen observed. "I'm sure he is using it as part of his curriculum for the abbeys."

Non spoke softly to the baby, "Dual identities come in handy these days. When you get bigger, we'll sneak you into the abbey so that you can learn how to be a Dragon flyer just like your mom and dad, and your dad's parents, and their parents' dad, and…"

Non remained with Cerridwen for the afternoon and helped her with chores while the baby slept. She washed the dishes, swept the floors, and wiped the baby clean. Then she left, promising to return another day to play with the baby. Cerridwen waved good-bye at the door. While the door was still ajar, another grandmother entered where the other had exited.

"Hi, dear!" Cerridwen's mother, a White fairy, said as she darted by her. "Where is my grandchild?"

"She's here, Mom, sleeping in the cradle," Cerridwen answered.

"Oh, she's beautiful!" the White fairy exclaimed, fluttering over the baby's head. "I'm so glad that you seduced Dewi."

"I didn't seduce him," Cerridwen said almost ruefully. "He jumped in the lake and swam after me." Then she added, "Mom, please don't wake the baby. I finally got her to sleep."

"Dewi is spouting poetry about how you seduced him. He even calls himself by another name. What is it now? Tell Lies Sin. No, it's Taliesin." Cerridwen's mother chuckled. "I knew that you two were destined to meet in an intimate manner when you received Pinkie as your dragon."

"I didn't seduce him, Mom," Cerridwen insisted. "I inspired him."

"What a divine inspiration!" Cerridwen's mother exclaimed with delight. She twirled in the air over the infant. "Oh yes, it was. Yes, it was. You can never be too good," she cooed over the child, who had just opened her eyes. The baby laughed delightedly at the fairy flying in her face. Creirwy tried to catch the White fairy in her chubby hands, but her dexterity was, fortunately, lacking. The White fairy continued, "Just what every princess needs, a fairy grandmother."

Cerridwen rolled her eyes and tossed her hands in the air. Then she collapsed in resignation, situating herself in a soft chair by the hearth. She watched the fairy and the baby play.

"She is going have quite the education," Cerridwen remarked.

"She is going to have the strength of a White fairy and the wisdom of her mama," the White fairy teasingly added. "Looks aren't everything, though you'll be an enchantress just like your mama."

"I'm not an enchantress," Cerridwen repeated. "When I'm not having babies, I work at the abbey as a nun. I counsel the sick and dying. You are going to give me a bad reputation."

"And the Enchantress of Lake Bala scares the cowardly Serpentines away," the White fairy said, ignoring her daughter. "Bad reputation, that's what Dewi and Grandma want. You and her are safer that way. We want to keep the Ceredigion Kingdom away from our babes, especially after they chased Dewi's mother, Non."

"I'm going to make some herb tea," Cerridwen sighed. "Would you like some nectar?"

"I'll pass. I ate on the way," the White fairy said, still swooping over the cradle far away from the infant's awkward grasp. "I haven't had this much fun since you were a baby. Human babies keep you busy."

Cerridwen smirked, vaguely recalling the games that she had played with her mother during her childhood. Like her early years with Dewi, the memories had been almost forgotten until now. She sipped her tea, savoring her own rebirth and transformation. So much had passed that had been unpleasant, leaving behind searing heartaches and grief. They were gone now, quickly evaporating in the swirling vortex of that day spent at Lake Bala. Fresh, happy memories were filling in the vacancies left by events best forgotten. She had ventured with Dewi past the veil separating life and death. Together, they had glimpsed the souls lighting the darkness of the portal dolmen within Pentre Ifan. They had been forever changed by the experience, which was as life-altering as the swim in Lake Bala. The souls around her at Pentre Ifan wanted to be remembered. They needed her help in their transformational journey so that they could move forward and return healed.

Cerridwen began to doze lightly as the fairy and infant entertained each other. So many deaths had passed already in her youth. With them had gone a piece of her heart, perhaps soul. Whatever she had witnessed in the portal dolmen was a reflected of her love for those who had departed. They represented the parts of her that needed to heal before they could return. As she drifted into a peaceful sleep, Cerridwen realized a renewal of her own spirit. It was time for a new beginning.